Taz let out
toward Millie, pulling up a smile
he hoped was both affectionate and
intimate.

His gaze locked on to hers, and he caught the flicker of panic she couldn't quite hide.

Better to rip the bandage off fast. Brutal, clean. Yes, this was an ambush, but this way he could take control of the narrative. Control was everything.

"Ladies and gentlemen," he began, keeping his tone smooth, "allow me to introduce Millie James. Not only does she manage my PR, but she's also my significant other." He let that land, enjoying the shocked gasps followed by stunned silence.

He rose to his feet, the scrape of the chair on the floor the only sound in the room. Then, taking his time, keeping it casual, he crossed the room to Millie. He cupped her cheek with one hand and brushed his mouth over hers—keeping the kiss soft, but deliberately possessive. He swallowed her shocked gasp, and her fingers trembled as he laced their fingers together.

"Let's go," he murmured against her ear, before pulling her toward the exit.

Joss Wood loves books, coffee and traveling—especially to the remote places of southern Africa and, well, anywhere. She's a wife and a mom to two young adults and is bossed around by two cats and a dog the size of a small cow. After a career in local economic development and business, Joss writes full-time from her home in KwaZulu-Natal, South Africa.

Books by Joss Wood

Harlequin Presents

Hired for the Billionaire's Secret Son
A Nine-Month Deal with Her Husband

Cape Town Tycoons

The Nights She Spent with the CEO
The Baby Behind Their Marriage Merger

A Diamond in the Rough

The Tycoon's Diamond Demand

Harlequin Desire

The Trouble with Little Secrets
Keep Your Enemies Close...

Visit the Author Profile page
at Harlequin.com for more titles.

FAST-TRACK
DATING DECEPTION

JOSS WOOD

PRESENTS

MIX
Paper | Supporting responsible forestry
FSC® C021394
www.fsc.org

Harlequin®
PRESENTS™

Recycling programs for this product may not exist in your area.

ISBN-13: 978-1-335-21356-3

Fast-Track Dating Deception

Copyright © 2026 by Joss Wood

Harlequin Enterprises ULC
22 Adelaide St. West, 41st Floor
Toronto, Ontario M5H 4E3, Canada
www.Harlequin.com

HarperCollins Publishers
Macken House, 39/40 Mayor Street Upper,
Dublin 1, D01 C9W8, Ireland
www.HarperCollins.com

Printed in Lithuania

FAST-TRACK
DATING DECEPTION

CHAPTER ONE

Shanghai

'HE'S LATE. WHY is he late?'

In the luxurious De Rossi hospitality suite above the pit lane at the Shanghai International Track, Millie James swallowed the urge to sarcastically ask Sylvie whether she'd *met* Taz De Rossi. Since starting work as Taz's press officer at the beginning of the Formula One season six weeks ago, he'd never been on time for anything PR-related. As the person responsible for managing his media requests and his public relations commitments, she spent a great deal of time apologising for him being late or for being a no-show. She didn't know why Sylvie expected Taz to attend this PR briefing for the De Rossi team; he hadn't attended any others so far this season.

The owner and principal driver of the famous F1 team never did anything he didn't want to do. And why should he? He came from a famous racing family and was on track to beat his older brother's record of three consecutive Formula One championship wins.

He was also, by far, the most difficult—if sexiest—client she'd ever worked with.

Arrogant, assured and annoying, but still *so* attractive.

Like her parents, he was one of life's golden people. Counting back, she realised she hadn't heard from them in many months. It was a measure of her discomfort that she found it easier thinking about her dysfunctional family than her very inconvenient attraction to her brusque boss.

Millie sighed. Her family...

It was impossible to think of her parents without thinking of her aunt and uncle—her mum and aunt were twins and lived two doors apart—as the quartet of semi-famous actors operated as an elegantly vicious pack. She and her cousin Ben, both only children, had been raised as siblings and had been extremely close, their bond fuelled by parental criticism, benign neglect and apathy. Ben often joked that they were shockingly well-adjusted considering they'd been raised by the four most self-involved people on planet Earth. To be fair, Ben had been less affected than Millie by their collective crazy.

It was true that the good died young...

Millie looked at the silver racing-car charm dangling from her heavy link silver bracelet. Over the past few months, as she inched closer to the tenth anniversary of Ben's death, she'd started questioning her life: who she was, what she wanted and where she was going. Ben's voice had been loud lately—*You're overqualified for your position as junior publicist, You should not have been passed over for that promotion, You're treading water.* He'd been the one person in her life who believed she was smart, capable and interesting.

In her late teens and early twenties, she'd ignored his offers to spend the weekend watching him race in glamorous cities and rejected his offers of free VIP race tickets. Her shyness and lack of confidence stopped her from visiting his sophisticated world. She'd been so convinced they had all the time in the world and would toast each other at their weddings and on milestone birthdays…until Ben had died in a horrific crash, and for years Millie ignored anything to do with Formula One racing.

Then she'd seen the press liaison position advertisement for De Rossi Racing, Ben's old Formula One team, and felt compelled to apply. Two months ago, she traded in her secure job as a junior accounts manager within a PR firm to take a ten-month contract with De Rossi Racing for the F1 season.

Despite hating the uncertainty of what she'd do after her contract ended, Millie never once second-guessed her decision. She needed to be here, in the world Ben loved, where his voice was loudest in her head, to make some hard decisions, including whether she saw herself as Ben did—capable, smart, interesting—or, as her parents did, boring and unadventurous. They were bold and beautiful, outrageously at ease standing in the spotlight. They craved attention and saw Millie's shyness and reserve as serious character flaws. In their eyes she was inadequate. *How did we create something so banal?* were their exact words.

Since Ben's death, she'd avoided them and her aunt and uncle as much as possible as she adjusted to the Ben-shaped hole in her life. Through avoidance, sheer grit and emotional distancing, she'd just managed to keep her head above choppy emotional waters. But the opportunity to be Taz De Rossi's press officer seemed to be a sign to stop treading water and start swimming. To move on, to change…to *live* by stepping into the world Ben—her best friend, her brother—had adored.

Mika, the team's senior public relations officer groaned and banged her phone against her forehead, jolting Millie out of her reverie. Millie recognised Mika's exasperation, as did Sylvie, who beat her to the punch. 'What has he done now?' she demanded.

Mika lifted her phone, and she and Sylvie took turns peering at the photographs on the screen. She recognised the club, Lily's, in London. In the photos, Taz was exiting the upmarket venue, a common occurrence. What made these photos newsworthy was that instead of walking out of the club with the always-volatile Phoebe, his on-off ex-model/influencer girlfriend, Taz held the hand of a stunning blonde.

Meredith, Taz's dead brother's fiancée, held her other hand up to her face, trying to shield her eyes from the blinding camera flashes. Taz looked like he wanted to hurt someone.

To be fair, he often looked like that. Unlike his brother Alex, who'd been charming, outgoing and gregarious, Taz's default expression was one of two: intimidating or brooding. And he had the face to pull it off: dark brown, almost black hair, laser-focused grey eyes, a long nose and high cheekbones. While Alex had been poster-boy pretty, Taz's face, with its severe angles, was harder, rougher and a great deal more masculine. Like a good painting, it was a face you could look at for a lifetime and still find it compelling.

But everyone knew Taz would never settle down. The notion was incomprehensible. He was the world's most eligible—and determined-to-remain-so—bachelor. He was selfish, a tad narcissistic and ruthlessly ambitious. Demanding, dismissive and difficult, he was very like

Millie's parents. There had been many times since starting work six weeks ago when she felt tongue-tied and
uncertain in his presence. She'd reminded herself she
was an adult and not the scared, shy and shunned child
standing in her parents' too-bright shadow.

In her personal life, she avoided Taz and people of his
ilk, bright and bold, effortlessly and innately confident.
Unfortunately, avoiding her employer wasn't an option.
Professionally, in PR terms, Taz was *messy*—and he was
her mess. 'What *does* Taz think he's doing?' Mika demanded. 'He knows Meredith is off-limits.'

'Do you think they went to the club together?' Sylvie
asked, frowning.

'Well, they certainly left it together,' Mika snapped
back. 'And according to gossip online, they spent most
of the evening snuggled up together in a booth.'

Millie took another look at the photograph. The six-
foot-two Taz, dressed in a white button-down with the
sleeves rolled up and dark blue jeans, towered over the
slim ex-model. His honed physique, wide shoulders, thick
arms and muscled legs made Meredith look even more
petite than she was. He was unquestionably attractive,
and he exuded an attitude of not caring what the world
thought about him.

She was the daughter of narcissistic, vain parents. She
wasted so much time wishing she could be the child they
wanted her to be, to reach what she now realised were
unrealistic expectations of her. She admired Taz's rebel-
lious, devil-may-care attitude. How nice it would be not
to care what people—including the semi-famous Quartet—thought.

Millie squinted at the picture… Something was off.

She wasn't getting the vibe that there was anything sexual about this encounter with the woman who'd been poised to be his sister-in-law. While she wasn't Taz's biggest fan, and he often made her job fifty times harder than it needed to be, she wasn't sure all was as it seemed.

'I'll show Taz the photo and ask for a comment,' Millie said. She wouldn't get one, but she'd ask.

Mika grimaced. 'I suggest you tiptoe through that minefield. Taz once threatened to fire me for asking about his love life. And Alex is never to be mentioned or discussed, *ever.*'

Alex had been racing royalty, Ben's best friend and racing teammate, but he'd died in a fluke accident seven years ago after slipping and smacking the back of his head on the corner of a marble kitchen counter. In internet chat rooms, fierce conspiracy theories raged over whether it was really an accident. Imagination, but no proof, was the only requirement needed to be a part of those discussions.

Two young men from the same racing team, both charismatic and confident, both top Formula One drivers, dead before their thirtieth birthdays. Life could be incomprehensibly awful on occasion.

Millie squinted. Something about the photo of Taz and Meredith still bothered her. Should she say anything? Did she have the right to comment? Would they listen? 'I…' she said.

Mika looked impatient at her hesitation. 'What?'

'I don't think they are dating,' Millie stated. 'Their fingers aren't interlocked. That's not how lovers hold hands. And he looks…worried.'

Sylvie sent her a thin-lipped smile. 'I think we know

him better than you, Millie. We've been working with Taz for more than a decade.'

It had been stupid to say anything, foolish to think they'd listen. They had known him longer, and she had only been working here a short time. But perhaps they also saw what they expected to see. He was the quintessential bad boy, and they expected bad-boy behaviour from him.

Millie looked down at her iPad as Mika and Sylvie stepped into the conference room. While she waited for Taz in the passage, she'd read through the briefing report and Taz's schedule on her tablet—not that he'd follow it. He had a press interview with an influential sports journalist at one thirty—he shouldn't miss that—and he needed to attend the FIA press conference. He had the sponsors' dinner at eight…

'How did you know that it wasn't a date?'

Taz's low, deep voice reached her ears, and Millie shuddered at the huff of his warm breath on her cheek. Shock kept her standing still; she hadn't heard him come up behind her. Heat rolled off him, along with his gorgeous cologne, something summer-fresh and sexy. She turned her head and noticed his bloodshot eyes and drawn face. It was obvious he'd had no sleep, and she wondered what or who had kept him up last night.

She hated the way he made her feel, shivery and shaky. Taz De Rossi made the world shift below her feet. Around him, she felt off balance, and it took all her mental energy not to let him see how much he affected her. His ego was big enough already.

And she had no experience in dealing with men who walked through the world with complete ease and confidence. The last man she dated—if two dinners could be called a date—was in his early forties, lived with his mum and was obsessed with video games. While she wasn't a virgin, she wasn't experienced.

Did experience matter? For her, marriage wasn't a long-term goal. Having grown up with the Quartet, she'd witnessed two highly dysfunctional, manipulative marriages, and she wasn't a fan. Besides, she still needed to unpack her emotional baggage and didn't have the mental fortitude to deal with someone else's.

Before she had the chance to answer, Taz jerked his head towards the hallway. 'Follow me.'

Yes, sir. Right away, sir. Millie cradled her iPad to her chest while Taz closed the door to the hospitality suite behind her. He moved further down the hallway, stopped and widened his stance. He crossed his arms across his wide chest, and Millie had to tip her head back to look into his harsh face. She wondered how he'd look with a smile on his face. She'd yet to see one.

'Good morning, Mr De Rossi,' she said, determined to be polite. Maybe one day he'd catch the hint and be polite back. But she wouldn't hold her breath. He didn't have anyone in his life brave enough, or important enough, to challenge him to change.

His eyes narrowed, his jaw tightened, and his lips thinned. Maybe she shouldn't poke the bear. She looked down at her screen. 'Can I run through today's schedule with you? The track walk is at ten, and the final seat fitting is at eleven. Then you have a *Fan Zone* appearance before lunch. You have an interview with—'

'Cancel it.'

His instruction wasn't unexpected, but it did make her

cross. He'd been messing the sports journalist around for weeks now, and she was losing patience. Millie didn't blame her. 'I don't think that's a good idea. She has a massive social media presence and is more influential than you probably realise.'

'A million followers across her platforms, with a demographic of twenty to thirty-five-year-olds,' Taz snapped back.

So he did listen to her. 'Then, why are you refusing to do the interview?'

His grey eyes burned into hers, and his mouth tightened, but he didn't answer. Not unexpected.

She'd try once more. Because getting him to do positive PR was her *job*. 'She told me that if you don't meet with her this time, she is going to run her story without your input.'

He lifted one broad shoulder. 'Let her.'

Millie sighed. Taz De Rossi didn't give a flying fig what people thought or wrote about him. He didn't only march to the beat of his own drum, he composed its music as well. Millie wanted to tell him he was being inconsiderate, disrespectful and rude. But, like her parents, Taz didn't care what she thought or felt. She was his employee, and he was her arrogant, egotistical and imperious boss, a man determined to make her job a thousand times harder than it needed to be.

And she'd never told anyone off in her life.

Thankfully, she wasn't as shy as she'd been as a teenager, and leaving home to go to university had helped her gain a little self-assurance. But she still tended to retreat into her shell when she felt uncomfortable, and Taz De Rossi made her feel very uncomfortable indeed. He was dauntless, so certain of his place in the world. In the face of people like him, she felt her self-confidence drain away. She straightened her shoulders and reminded herself that she'd taken this job, joined the De Rossi team, to do something different, to *be* different. She wanted to change her outlook and her life because she was tired of coasting, wondering whether there was more to life, more to *her*. To push, as Ben had always wanted her to, through her cocoon of self-doubt. Ben had been so convinced that she was bolder, braver and more self-assured than she believed herself to be. Millie's way of honouring him, ten years later, was to find out whether he was right or not.

It was proving to be a one-step-forward-three-steps-back situation, but six weeks in, she was still working for Taz De Rossi. She'd count that as a win. 'Cancel the interview,' Taz reiterated. 'I'm not in the mood to make nice with journalists.'

To be fair, he never was. Millie sighed and nodded, hoping the journalist wouldn't shoot the messenger. 'I'll walk the track, and I'll do the seat fitting,' Taz's words shot out, bullet-fast.

Of course he would. Despite being at the top of his game and being familiar with the track, Taz would still inspect it with his race and performance engineers and his race strategist. Winning his fourth consecutive championship was all that mattered, and he was on record as saying he'd do anything and everything to make that happen. Interviews, PR and making nice with the sponsors and his brand partners were way down on his list of priorities.

Now for the hard bit... 'There's a lot of buzz about you and Meredith. How would you like us to handle it?'

His gaze pinned her feet to the ground. 'How do you

think I want you to handle it?' he asked, his tone silky with disdain.

'By not responding to it?'

'So why did you bother to ask?' His voice remained low but edged in steel.

It was a good question. Millie looked around for an answer, but the empty corridor, uninteresting and silent with its polished floors and stark lighting, held no answers. She swallowed, conscious of Taz's cool confidence, so sure the world would accommodate itself to his will. He didn't move or speak, but he didn't need to. Wherever he went, his sheer presence demanded complete attention, and Millie wasn't immune. She remained immobile, her composure wavering under the intensity of his stare.

Why was he looking at her like that?

He was, she frantically reminded herself, a Formula One legend.

Untouchable. Ruthless. Relentless.

His eyes remained locked on her face, her body still tightened beneath his scrutiny, and baby fireworks erupted over her skin. Electricity ran through her, down her spine and out of her toes. Her heart flip-flopped around her ribcage, and her stomach vibrated. And where had all the moisture in her mouth gone? Did he have to stand so close? And why was her stomach suddenly doing somersaults?

Judging by his narrowed eyes and the infinitesimal hint of a smug smile from lips perpetually set in either a smirk or a scowl, he was very aware of his effect on her. She cursed her treacherous body for liking his and him for knowing that it did. After another tense few seconds,

Millie wrenched her eyes away and stared down again at her tablet.

She was, she reminded herself, here to figure out her life, not to date. She did not need the complication of having any kind of feelings for her boss.

It galled her to admit that whenever she thought of dating, Taz's tough face flashed before her eyes. Something beyond his good looks and aura of capability and confidence intrigued her. He was the human version of the Chinese nesting boxes she'd seen sightseeing yesterday. Which box held the authentic version of Taz De Rossi? No one knew, certainly not her. And it didn't matter because he was…

Out. Of. Her. League.

He would never ask her out; she would never accept. But it was a universal law of life that people like him, people like her parents, didn't look down, they looked up or around. Like, after all, attracted like. The reality was that in today's world, there was an unspoken status system, a psychological way of pushing people into their lane. The rich and beautiful occupied one top echelon, and so it went down in layers of beauty, charm and wealth. It was how the world worked, and anyone who thought being rich and beautiful didn't put you in a position of power was naive. Of course it did.

Millie pushed her thoughts away: It was time for her to get back to work. But more than anything, she needed distance from Taz. When she wasn't around him, she was sane and rational. When she was within twenty yards of him, lust-coated stupidity lived in her head rent free alongside questions like why he acted the way he did and why he, on some level, intrigued her. Why did she keep hoping for more beyond his haughty attitude and stop-the-traffic looks? Why was she hunting for a hint of authenticity?

Enough, Millie. He's a lost cause.

She turned to walk away, but his hand shot out, gripped her elbow and stopped her in her tracks. She turned to face him and raised her eyebrows. 'You didn't answer my question.'

Her pulse quickened. 'Which one?' she said, pretending she didn't understand.

He stared at her, calling her bluff. Millie rubbed the back of her neck. He wasn't going to let her walk away until she gave him an answer to his original question about Meredith. 'Uh, you looked protective, not...um... turned-on. I saw it in the way you held Meredith's hand.'

Confusion raced across his face. 'The way I held her hand?'

Millie locked her fingers together. 'Lovers hold their hands linked this,' she said as she demonstrated. 'You held her hand like you would hold the hand of a daughter or sister.'

'Pretty observant,' he stated.

She tipped her head to the side and noticed curiosity in his eyes.

No, she *had* to be imagining it.

'It's my job to analyse the way the media covers you, just like it's my job to keep you on message.' She kept her tone crisp and professional, ignoring the way her body tightened beneath his scrutiny.

He didn't move a muscle, but it felt like he'd leaned in, closer than he was before. 'So how's that working out for you?' he asked, his voice husky, the tiniest glint of humour in his pewter-coloured eyes.

They both knew the answer to his question was *Badly*. Millie released a heavy sigh, and beneath the dark scruff edging his lips his mouth curved into a super-swift, able-to-melt-glass smile. So that was what it felt like to touch a lightning bolt.

Millie suppressed the urge to check whether anyone was standing behind her. This was the first time he'd said anything even vaguely personal to her, had instigated conversation. Was he toying with her? She wrinkled her nose and rocked on her heels, uncomfortable. Was she judging him harshly because his confidence, charisma and success triggered the same feelings of inadequacy as her parents' did? Was it easier to think poorly of him?

Millie looked past Taz to the door to the hospitality suite. 'I should get back in there.'

When he didn't say anything, she skirted his big frame and put her hand on the door-handle. As she started to open the door, Taz spoke. 'It's not your job to defend me, and I don't appreciate you gossiping about my private life.'

Millie stiffened, and heat climbed up her neck and into her face.

'Do it again and you will be fired.'

Yes, there was the demanding ass who paid her salary.

CHAPTER TWO

ON SUNDAY, RACE-DAY, Millie stood at the back of the De Rossi hospitality suite, her eyes on the huge screen in front of her. She could've gone down to the paddock to watch the race, but, like most sports, you got better coverage by watching and listening to the race on the TV.

She pulled her De Rossi–branded black-and-pink polo shirt off her clammy body. She'd tucked the shirt into her favourite black skinny jeans and wore high-top black trainers because being on her feet for long stretches made her feet ache. She'd pulled her mass of curls into a haphazard bun on the top of her head and had bitten off all her lipstick long ago.

Watching a race wasn't her favourite thing to do—a result of Ben's deadly crash at the Imola Circuit—but she didn't usually have such a tight knot in her stomach or a lump in her throat. Why did she feel like she was waiting for an axe to fall? Sure, Taz had been in a filthy mood since Thursday, biting off heads and stripping skin, but that wasn't unusual. He wasn't a sunshine-and-roses guy, and she'd learned not to take his moods personally. How could she when she spent minimal time with him? So why was she feeling so uptight, so incredibly tense? What was wrong with her?

Millie kept her eyes fixed on the TV screen, which showed Taz had an extensive lead over the rest of the field. She continued to be impressed at his total control of a projectile speeding down the track at three hundred-plus miles per hour. It took intelligence, guts and incredible reflexes to handle the multimillion-dollar car. Racers required a warrior-like attitude, lots of verve and a certain amount of arrogance to be world champions.

Taz roared up to a slower car, one he was lapping and veered right to overtake. The driver of the other car, a rookie driver according to the race announcer, tried to tuck himself in behind Taz as they approached a sharp corner, and he touched his brakes a millisecond too late. His front fender clipped the back of Taz's car and sent both cars spinning across the track. Millie lifted her clenched fists to her mouth, praying neither car would hit a barrier. Eventually both cars stopped, and everyone in the room, in the pit, on the stands and watching around the world on millions of screens let out a collective sigh of relief. Because the drivers reached impossible speeds, safety was paramount in Formula One. Everyone knew serious injury or death was a possibility.

But not today, not with Taz. But there was no chance of him winning the Shanghai race now. It was okay: He could afford to lose a race or two. But she knew that wouldn't matter to him. Winning was everything.

Millie slumped, tuning out the curses at the rookie driver, the aspersions cast on his driving and his team. Closing her eyes, she hauled in a couple of deep breaths, grateful Taz wasn't hurt. Was she shaking because his crash reminded her of the deadly injuries Ben sustained when he went careening off the track? Maybe.

The sport was exciting, but it was also exceedingly dangerous.

The volume of noise rose. Millie opened her eyes and, on the screen, saw Taz's car limping into the pits below them. The car door opened, and Taz climbed out and ripped off his helmet. The camera zoomed in on his face, and Millie caught his deep frown and bright eyes. Fury rolled off him in waves.

Ignoring his mechanics, he stomped out of the pit and half jogged down the concourse, the cameras following his progress to the rookie driver's pit. The race announcer's voice sped up, his words nearly indistinguishable as Taz stormed up to the driver. There was no doubt he knew his mistake had cost Taz the race.

Taz called his name, and the rookie winced, panic evident on his face. The next few seconds were a blur as Taz lifted the rookie to his toes and backed him into the wall. Millie watched, stunned, as Taz yelled at him. Taz ignored the hands pulling him away, but when a burly mechanic wrapped his beefy arm around Taz's waist and hauled him off, Taz finally backed down. The cameras panned in, and Millie caught his ultra-brief what-the-hell-am-I-doing expression before his frown returned. He batted away the mechanic and, as if making a point, punched the wall next to the rookie's shoulder. Dropping his hand, he stalked away, his head held high and his eyes blazing.

Millie rubbed the back of her neck and grimaced. Well, if he was in a bad mood before, he was going to be in a worse one now.

Coming down from a massive adrenaline spike, Taz left the pit and stalked into his driver's room, slamming the door behind him. To make sure he wasn't disturbed, he twisted the lock and headed to the small bar fridge behind a cupboard door. He pulled out a bottle of water, cracked it open and drank it down. Tossing the empty bottle into a trash can, he drained another before reaching for the bottle of Macallan he'd stashed away in another cupboard. He removed the lid and took a hefty swig straight from the bottle before pouring three fingers into a glass. Sure, whisky wasn't on the dietician's list of approved food and drinks, but right now, he didn't give a damn. His arms ached from steering, and his neck was tense from holding his head upright in the corners.

He was exhausted. And he'd messed up. Badly.

Taz sat on his leather couch and rested his forearms on his knees, the whisky bottle dangling from his hand. He'd allowed his temper to override good sense today, and he would have a price to pay for his loss of control. He would, at the very least, face censure from the officials, maybe even a race ban.

He pushed his finger and thumb into his eye sockets and cursed. He had a good lead over his arch-rival, but it would quickly be erased if he wasn't allowed to compete. When he returned, he'd have to fight for the title, harder than he'd expected to. He'd put blood in the water, and the sharks were swirling.

Losing his temper had been moronic, and at thirty-five, he knew better. Was better. Even if the rest of the world didn't see it. Even if he didn't let them see it.

Taz took another sip of whisky, recapped the bottle and placed it on the floor. He'd had a couple of awful days, but today's crash was a highlight. He should've accelerated faster and made allowances for the rookie's inexperience. But, because he'd allowed his attention to drift, he hadn't.

When his two main rivals had retired earlier in the race, one with an engine failure and one after a crash at the start, he'd gone on autopilot, doing what he did best while allowing his brain to wander into territory it shouldn't have while guiding a bullet around a twisty track. He'd been driving from muscle memory and experience, with thoughts of his press officer drifting in and out. He didn't give anyone that privilege, that mental space, not when he was racing. So why Millie?

She wasn't glamorous, nothing like the sophisticated women he slept with. A spray of freckles covered her nose and cheeks, and in the sunlight her honey-coloured curls held hints of strawberry. Her mouth was full and wide, her chin stubborn and her body curvy. The slight rasp in her voice set his nerve endings alight.

But her far-too-beguiling looks weren't his only distraction. He'd remembered how she defended him the other day, for standing up for him when everyone else assumed he was dating Meredith. When was the last time someone had spoken up on his behalf? His mum, maybe? Sometime before her death shortly after he turned five? He genuinely couldn't remember and didn't think his father or brother ever did that for him. He was, after all, the family afterthought, the spare to the heir, ignored and neglected. He was the owner of this team, and the principal driver, only through death and fate.

If Alex hadn't died, sending their father into a spiral of despair that had led to a series of strokes, he might still be the De Rossi family outcast. Not worthy enough to take a seat at the table.

On the track, while overtaking the rookie, he'd been thinking of how nice it was to have someone standing in his corner, if only for a minute, imagining how it would feel to have someone like Millie, someone genuine, standing by his side supporting him. A second later he heard the thud and started to spin.

He'd risked everything, put his all-consuming goal of winning his fourth championship in jeopardy because he'd lost focus, because Millie hadn't, like everyone else, jumped to conclusions about him. Because she'd looked deeper beyond the image the world had of him. Not that he'd done anything to challenge the public's perception of him... If anything he'd gone out of his way to perpetuate the myth of being unapologetically confident, brazenly selfish and boldly carefree. He'd rather be hated than pitied, loathed than looked down on.

Nothing came between him and what he needed to do on the track, and he was mortified, furious that he'd let a woman—his press liaison officer, for God's sake—get under his skin. What was wrong with him?

He didn't need her or anyone's validation. He was Tazio De Rossi, and nobody warranted an explanation of his behaviour. Besides, would anyone believe that his running into Meredith at the club had been a coincidence? Probably not, but he would never have *chosen* to spend four hours listening to her talk about Alex. Seven years had passed, but to Meredith his death had happened yesterday.

And that was why he normally avoided her, and why he never displayed any pictures of Alex, not here or at any of his houses. He couldn't stand reminders of the brother his father loved so much. All his life he'd been compared to Alex, with his father telling him he wasn't as smart, as nice, as charming or as good-looking. That he would never be as good a driver…

When he died, Alex was feted as the darling of the racing world, a devoted fiancé, a super-involved philanthropist and a regular on talk shows where he was renowned for his wit and charm. Taz wondered what his legions of fans would think if they knew the truth…

On the surface, it was simple: a horrible, tragic accident, something no one could've predicted. The press had recounted the events accurately: During the F1 summer break, Alex flew to New York City for a long weekend, while his long-time fiancée Meredith attended a bachelorette party in Rome. While staying at the family's brownstone mansion Alex, wearing socks, rushed to answer his ringing phone and slipped. On his way down, he cracked his head on the sharp corner of the Italian marble slab covering the island in the gourmet kitchen. He died on impact.

Everyone, F1 fans or not, agreed Alex's death had been heartbreaking.

Later that night, Matteo De Rossi had suffered the first of a series of strokes. The last one would take his life just two years later.

When Taz visited his father in hospital the day after Alex's death, Matteo's high-priced lawyer briefed him. There had been a breakdown of communication between Matteo and Alex: Both had thought the house would be unoccupied that weekend. Matteo heard a woman screaming and came downstairs to find a half-dressed teenager on her knees next to Alex, her hand on his chest. He'd seen rows of cocaine on the island counter and liquor bottles on the coffee table in the lounge area adjacent to the kitchen. The girl—still a month short of eighteen—was Mount Everest–high. Knowing Alex was dead, Matteo called his lawyer instead of 911 and the police. The lawyer arrived and removed the girl, the drugs and all traces of their private party.

Only when the brownstone was clean and empty, the threat to Alex's reputation neutralised, were the police called. The story Matteo told was simple: He'd come downstairs for a drink, saw Alex and called 911. He held himself together, and at three in the morning he collapsed while talking to his lawyer and was rushed to hospital.

When he regained consciousness days later, his first and only demand was that Alex's *indiscretions* had to remain a family secret. And so it did. Five years had passed since Matteo's death, but only he and the lawyer knew the truth about that night. After going through Alex's phone and laptop, they discovered that drug-fuelled orgies with under-age girls was a favourite pastime. Given his high profile, how he'd never been outed was a complete mystery.

Was Taz's anger and bitterness compounded by the fact that his father, even after Alex's death, continued to denigrate and dismiss him, while extolling Alex's virtues in public and in private? Alex, a larger-than-life figure before his untimely death, became almost godlike in death. Taz often fought the urge to scream the truth, to tell the world that the perfect Alex was anything but. But he kept quiet and remained in the shadows cast by his brilliant brother.

Taz scrubbed his hands over his face. Something had shut down in him the night of Alex's death. Years had passed, yet he still felt like he was encased in ice, watching the world from a distance and unable to break free. And the only way he could step into the light was to beat Alex's record of three driver championships in a row. He knew he'd never be as popular, as universally adored, as his brother. He didn't need to be. But if he beat Alex's record, the world would see him as the better F1 driver. In the competition between him and Alex, it was the only prize up for grabs.

But he'd torpedoed that goal by losing his temper with the rookie driver. What the *hell* had he been thinking? He knew better than that! He *was* better than that. But he'd been caught in a storm of resentment, fear and fury. The kid had been a handy target...

His actions in the pit were wholly unacceptable. Not only was he one of the senior drivers on the circuit but he was also a role model to the younger drivers. And the owner of a team. He was, not for the first time, ashamed of his actions. He needed to apologise privately to his colleague and publicly to the racing world and his fans.

He'd messed up before, but nothing as serious as this. And it had happened because he'd allowed his attention to wander to his press liaison officer.

Taz shoved his fingers into his hair. He'd put his championship in jeopardy, and he'd risked everything he was working for.

It was completely and wholly unacceptable. And it stopped right now.

He put his hand on the arm of the chair and tried to push himself up but nearly fainted as hot, searing pain rolled from the tips of his fingers, down the back of his hand and into his wrist. He sat again, and when the black dots disappeared from behind his eyes, he lifted his injured hand and noticed his swollen blue-black fingers and bloody knuckles. The bruise extended down his hand and covered his wrist. He'd broken a finger, maybe cracked his hand, his wrist. *Shit.* He was in a world of trouble here.

Pushing himself to his feet, hissing from the pain, he walked over to the door, flipped the lock and eyed the group waiting in the hallway. His CEO, his technical director, the team's long-time race engineer and, behind them, his PR team. Including Millie.

He gripped the door-frame and caught the sympathy in her purple-blue eyes, along with a healthy dose of exasperation. He could brush off his team's frustration and anger—he didn't care about their approval or disapproval—but for some reason, he cared what his press liaison officer thought about him. It was not an emotion he liked or was familiar with.

He kept his expression cold. 'I take it my actions made the news?' he asked sarcastically.

His race engineer was the first to speak. 'Alex would never—'

No, he couldn't deal with any references to Alex right now.

'Not now, Len,' he snapped. No matter what he did or how long he lived, he'd never manage to live up to Saint Alex's legacy.

He looked at his CEO. 'Any word from the disciplinary committee?'

'Nothing official, but it's not going to be good.'

Taz looked down at his rapidly swelling hand.

'You do realise that you have wiped out any advantage you had, don't you?' Len persisted. 'You will have to win most of the races going forward and hope your competitors mess up.'

Yes, he'd already run the scenarios and reached that conclusion. He rubbed his uninjured hand over his face, met Millie's eyes and saw the worry in hers and the way they kept darting to his swollen hand. He considered his predicament. Not least how he was going to navigate the next few weeks of his life one-handed—without allowing anyone into his inner sanctum. He would never do that. Even when he slept with a woman, he always went to her place, and his driver room and hotel suite were solidly off-limits to everyone, his safe spaces. That was why he was holding this meeting in a hallway.

But he needed professional help to navigate the bad press heading his way. This wasn't a situation he could fix on his own. The thought settled like a wet, heavy blanket, unfamiliar and deeply uncomfortable. Relying on others wasn't in his nature. He thrived on self-sufficiency, answered to no one and carved his own path. That's what happened when your father and brother thought of you as surplus to requirements. He was perfectly content in his emotional isolation.

But this situation needed PR expertise and someone he could trust. He recalled the way Millie had considered the photo of him and Meredith. Instead of jumping to conclusions, she'd looked deeper. Given him the benefit of the doubt. He couldn't remember the last time anyone had done that. He needed someone in his life who could look past his reputation and his brother's achievements, someone who saw *him*. Someone he could work with…

From somewhere he also recalled hearing that Millie

had left her job at a PR firm in London to work as his press liaison officer. So she clearly knew her stuff.

Decision made.

'I'm promoting Millie from being my press liaison officer to being my PR officer. You need to speak to me, go through her.'

Millie's mouth fell open as a chorus of disapprovals rose in the hallway. She looked as shocked as everyone else. Tough.

'Millie, get the team doctor up here.'

'Um… I think we need to discuss this,' Millie said, with more than a little panic in her voice.

He was tired, he felt like he'd been hit by a truck, and his hand was on fire. 'Doctor, *now*.' Then he stepped back into his room and slammed the door, welcoming the silence.

He walked over to the couch and lay down on it, gently resting his injured hand on his flat stomach and placing his other forearm over his eyes.

How was he going to dig himself out of this hole?

CHAPTER THREE

MUCH LATER THAT NIGHT, Millie slipped inside Taz's private hospital room, wincing at the plaster encasing his hand from the tips of his fingers to an inch below his elbow. A few hours after the team doctor looked at the X-ray of his hand, he was wheeled into a state-of-the-art theatre and had the best orthopaedic surgeon in China operating on his hand. Now his cast lay next to him on the bed and his other hand cupped the back of his head. His eyes were closed and he didn't look like he was in pain.

Millie hesitated. She didn't know Taz well enough to visit him in the hospital, to be in his room so late at night, but she needed to ask how he wanted her to respond to the incessant demands from reporters desperate for a comment, update or interview. If he'd threatened to fire her for sharing her thoughts on a photo, taking the initiative and putting out a press release without Taz's approval was surely a fireable offence.

But as much as she wished she could say that she was here solely as his press officer, she couldn't. Since their conversation in the corridor, she'd felt unsettled and unsure why. Working for Taz had always been a challenge—demanding, relentless—but manageable. Her attraction to him had been little more than a quiet hum beneath the surface. That vague hum was now a strong current—sharp and impossible to ignore. Why did she suddenly feel super aware around him? What had changed between them? Was she being overly imaginative? Highly possible.

During the race, she'd been on edge, hyper aware, waiting for something—anything—to happen. And it had. He crashed, lost his temper and then, out of nowhere, announced her promotion. It floored her, and she didn't understand it. Neither did anyone else. But as she stood in the doorway, she froze. His closed eyes and pale face suggested this wasn't the time. He was injured, and she and everyone else could wait.

She turned to tiptoe out, but then Taz's deep voice floated across the room. 'Millie.'

She wrinkled her nose. *Busted.* Millie looked down, but instead of sporting glassy eyes and a loopy smile he looked fully alert. 'How long have you been out of the theatre?' she asked.

'Two or so hours,' he replied. 'What are you doing here?'

Millie jammed her hands into the back pockets of her jeans and rocked from side to side. 'The press is all over you for pushing the rookie driver, and they are not being kind. I need to know how you want me to mitigate any possible damage to your brand. And I really need to talk to you about my unexpected promotion.'

He looked at the cast on his hand. 'And this couldn't wait until morning?'

'Well, the sooner I start spinning the story, the sooner this will blow over.'

'Again, it could've waited.'

Millie shuffled on her feet. She couldn't tell him the

third and last reason she was here. It was super simple: She wanted to see how he was and felt compelled to visit him because she didn't think any of his staff would bother. Taz was their boss, and they respected him, but she knew they didn't particularly like him. But nobody should be alone after an operation. Not even the incredibly self-sufficient Taz De Rossi.

'Are you in any pain?' she asked, walking over to stand next to his bed.

'Despite the anaesthetic and the drugs, I feel remarkably clear-headed.' His lips curved into a disarming smile. He looked so much younger when he smiled. 'And pain-free.'

When the meds wore off, his injured hand would let itself be known. 'What did they do?' she asked, nodding to his hand.

'Put in a pin to stabilise my middle finger,' he replied. 'I also have a minor crack in my wrist. I punched that wall pretty hard, but they both should heal within four to six weeks. It wasn't my finest hour.'

Millie lifted her eyebrows at his self-criticism. It had been a foolish thing to do, but she'd never expected Taz to admit it. It was late, the hospital ward was quiet, his private room felt like a cocoon, and Millie felt like they were the only two people around. His navy T-shirt— no hospital gown for Taz De Rossi—covered his broad chest and hugged his muscular shoulders, and his cast was blindingly white against his tanned upper arm. His stubble was thicker, his grey eyes tired but still sharp. Assessing. It would take more than a high-speed crash, a media PR disaster and an operation to make Taz De Rossi break out in a sweat.

'How bad is the fallout? On a scale of one to ten?'

She considered lying but lifted one shoulder instead. 'Twelve?'

He cursed. 'And what have the stewards decided?'

'They are still discussing it and said they'd send an email first thing in the morning.'

He pulled a face. 'If it needs that much discussion, then I'm in trouble.'

Frankly, he was. His actions had been broadcast to millions of people around the world. At best he'd lost his temper and was a bully, at worst he'd resorted to violence. Either way, team owner or not, high profile or not, he wasn't the poster boy for good sportsmanship.

'It's been a rough day,' Taz murmured, the king of the understatement

She agreed. He was difficult and reticent and frequently rude, but his day had gone from bad to worse to edging into catastrophic.

'And unfortunately the next few days will be as bad, if not worse. If the stewards came back with a rest-of-the-season ban, that's it for the season. And there will be no way I can beat—'

He stopped speaking and turned his head away, but not before Millie caught the apprehension in his eyes and the panic on his face. It was the first time she'd seen his I've-got-everything-control façade slip. Seeing that chink in his armour made him seem more attractive—if that was even possible.

And dangerous. So dangerous. She needed to keep *not* liking him so she didn't do anything rash like make her attraction to him known. She felt like she'd already lost ground to him; she couldn't surrender anymore.

She looked at the door and tried to smile. 'I'm going to go. I'll be back in the morning. As I said, there are things we need to discuss, including this promotion you dropped in my lap—'

'Most people would be happy to be promoted.'

If they thought they could handle the job, sure, then happiness was warranted. But Millie had her doubts. She'd only ever handled small accounts, and Taz had the eyes of the world on him. This was a job for the best in the business, not for an inexperienced woman working out who she was, what she wanted and how she should walk through the world.

'As I said, we need to discuss it.' She shouldn't be here: It was inappropriate, and he looked tired. 'But it can wait until morning.' She looked at the closed door. 'I should go.'

'Wait,' Taz replied. He lifted his free hand to grip her upper arm. He tugged her down so that her mouth was an inch away from his, and his breath warmed her lips. 'You don't like me very much, do you?'

Up until Thursday, she hadn't. Or not much. Like her parents, he was ridiculously arrogant and entirely too used to getting his way. But something had shifted, leaving her disoriented and off balance.

It was as if she'd slipped on a new pair of glasses and suddenly, the world—*he*—had come into sharper focus. Maybe it was the lines of pain etched into his face, his tired eyes or the white cast, but his hard edges now seemed less jagged, the aloofness less tangible, his loneliness palpable. She felt rattled: She wasn't ready for anything to change between them.

Like him, she was weary. It had been a long day, and

she was emotionally and physically drained. It was natural to overthink *everything*...

'Are those drugs finally kicking in?' she asked, changing the subject.

'I'm fine.' The side of his mouth lifted in a half smile. 'You don't need to answer, I can see it in your eyes. Few people like me, and I can live with that.'

She wanted to deny his words, but a sense of self-preservation held her back. What was the point of admitting that he fascinated her? There could never be anything between them. He was a shooting star, and she was...*not*.

Taz had made being emotionally unavailable into an art form. 'I don't think you let people close enough to decide whether they like you or not.'

His eyebrows rose at that assessment, but instead of responding he tipped his head to the side, his hand still on her arm. 'But you do want me to kiss you. You're attracted to me.'

His words were softly uttered but no less powerful than a shout. He was an experienced guy, and she'd been foolish to think he hadn't picked up on her attraction, wouldn't be surprised to hear that, whenever he was close or within twenty feet of her, she felt like she'd been struck by lightning. Thoughts of how it would feel to have her lips under his, to skim his hard, muscled body with her hands, consumed her.

Attracted was too tame a word to describe her reaction to him. The truth was, in this moment, she'd never wanted anyone more. She burned for him, and she wasn't a woman who liked playing with fire. *Why did he make her feel like this?*

Millie held her breath as Taz's hand moved up her arm

and slid around the back of her neck. He tunnelled his long fingers into her hair. She knew she should be sensible and pull back and put some distance between them. But she was so tired of being sensible, of doing what was expected. She wanted to step into the fire and feel the flames lick her face. Kissing him was a very bad idea, but she was, strangely and uncharacteristically, going to do it anyway.

Taz lifted his mouth and pulled her head down, and their lips met in a kiss that was as soft as it was sexy. She placed her fingers on his jaw, surprised at the softness of the stubble on his jaw and cheek. It tickled her lips as he explored her mouth, his tongue pressing the seam of her lips, demanding entrance.

She shouldn't—he was her boss, for God's sake! He paid her salary. She shouldn't even be here, in this hospital room, with him. But her body, more specifically her mouth, failed to decode her brain's frantic messages. Her lips parted, partly from shock, partly from need, and he slipped inside her mouth, setting off a chain reaction of baby fireworks on her skin. His tongue tangled with hers, and she heard his rumble of appreciation and felt his hand tightening on her head. Her blood heated, her eyes closed, and she never wanted him to stop. This was, bar none, the best kiss of her life…

His soft grumble, deep in his throat released the last string holding her control together, and the fingers of her hand speared into his hair, and her other hand pulled his soft T-shirt up his stomach to find warm male skin. All she wanted to do was to straddle him, rock herself against his hard length. Why was she reacting like this? Who *was* she? Why did he make her feel so reckless?

And breathless.

His hand ran up and down her back, over her hip, up her ribcage. It wasn't nearly enough. Nothing but being naked and having him inside her would be enough. Millie didn't recognise herself: She never responded like this, was never needy and…*wanton*.

Men never made her feel wild and out of control. Taz, through some dark magic, did.

And boy, did he know how to use his lips. Was he as good at making love as he was at kissing? Of course he would be: He'd had lots of practice with a steady stream of women. But knowing what type of woman he usually went for—slim, sophisticated, *famous*—why was he kissing her?

Except that he wasn't. Kissing her. Not anymore. His lips weren't moving, and his hand fell from her head to his side. Millie pulled back. His eyes slammed into hers, and she thought she caught shock in his, echoed by his bobbing Adam's apple. She straightened, and Taz rested his head on his pillow and pushed his hand through his messy hair.

If he was anyone but Taz De Rossi, she would suspect he was a little off balance and that he'd been caught off guard by the heat of their kiss. But that wasn't feasible. He closed his eyes, and his thick lashes lay against his pale skin. The lines of pain were deeper now, and he pressed his lips together.

'Are your pain meds wearing off?' she asked. She had to say something, the silence between them excruciating.

'Yeah,' he replied, his voice a little rough.

It was a perfectly reasonable explanation: He'd had a high-speed crash and an operation. But Millie wasn't buying it. She was starting to read his body language, and his tight lips and the muscle jumping in his jaw suggested something was bubbling under the surface. She was tempted to push but decided not to. Did she want to know? Could she handle it if she did?

It was late and so much had happened, there was no need to toss an accelerant on a runaway fire.

Maybe their kiss was simply an unusual end to an unusual day. She shouldn't read anything into it. He might not even remember it in the morning. And if he did, he would probably, hopefully, write it off as a spur-of-the-moment thing.

God, she hoped so. Millie left his room, shut the door behind her, plopped down in the nearest chair in the hallway and rested her forehead on her fist.

A normal Sunday night back in London meant a curry in front of the TV, maybe folding some laundry, vacuuming her flat if she felt energetic. But here she was sitting in a hospital in Shanghai, newly promoted to a job she didn't think she could do, reliving a kiss with her boss.

Who *was* she?

And that was the issue, wasn't it? That was why she was here. Because she didn't want to be who she was, but didn't know who she wanted to be. Or who she could be. She needed a new version of herself, a Millie 2.0, but had no idea what that person looked like or what she believed. About the world or herself.

When she was younger, she'd been intimidated by the sophisticated and wealthy world of F1 racing, by the sophisticated girls Ben dated, the circles he socialised in, and the wealth and the luxury surrounding him. Both her and Ben's parents glittered and glowed, and they'd easily slid into Ben's world and navigated it with ease. Unlike the rest of her family, she didn't like the spotlight.

Her parents had only ever planned on having one child. Another child would've demanded more—time, money and input—than they were prepared to offer, but they'd been vastly disappointed in the child they got. They'd told her, quite often, that they felt cheated she wasn't confident, charming or talented enough to share their limelight, to be loved.

It had been the same for Ben until his racing career took off and he started building a reputation at De Rossi Racing. His friendship with Alex De Rossi hadn't hurt and had boosted his profile further. His parents and hers had welcomed him back into the family like the prodigal son. Was her refusal to join Ben at his races, to step into his glamorous and sophisticated world, motivated by her anger and resentment that he was successful and popular and therefore acceptable and valuable to his parents and hers?

Maybe? Her insecure behaviour aside, Ben always reminded her that she was strong, lovely and smart and could hold her head up wherever she went, with whoever she met. He was the only one who saw her doing and being more…

Weirdly, in some strange and expected way, Taz promoting her and then kissing her made her feel the same way. That maybe she could do hard or unexpected things, handle more responsibility and…

And that she was more attractive than she believed herself to be. That she mattered.

No, she was being naive and making unfounded assumptions. The world didn't work that way. Her promotion was likely to be rescinded in the morning when Taz had some time to review his impulsive decision. He'd only kissed her because he'd been half-asleep and was a little woozy from the anaesthetic. It meant nothing: He'd been acting on instinct.

'Is everything all right?'

Millie jumped at the sound of a nurse's voice, and jerked her head up, her hand on her heart. 'Sorry, you frightened me.'

'You look tired.'

Millie *was* emotionally and physically exhausted. It had been a day.

'Maybe you should go now.'

Millie nodded, picked up her bag, slung it crossways across her chest and looked at Taz's closed door. She thought she should say something, ask the nurse to keep an eye on him, but that was stupid and unnecessary. She was his *employee*, not his girlfriend.

She needed to remember that. She had things to do, and falling for her attractive boss wasn't on the agenda.

Taz heard the door snick shut and lifted his good arm and placed it across his eyes. Spikes of pain ran up his other arm and into his shoulder, and all he wanted was the oblivion of drug-induced sleep. Or Millie's lips back on his.

While he'd kissed her, he'd forgotten everything in his life, totally lost in her heat and her mouth. The agony of his injury faded, humiliation lessened, and his anxiety about the championship dissipated. He'd been utterly, wholly into her: her light, feminine perfume, the softness of her hair, her glorious mouth.

His harsh F-bomb shattered the silence of his private room. Maybe the drugs and anaesthetic had affected him more than he realised. Because women, especially a woman like Millie—a little unsure, not-so-sophisticated, very real—didn't make him feel like this. Off-kilter. Out of control.

He liked being alone. He'd embraced self-sufficiency because it was easier to stand by himself than to be disappointed and abandoned, to be shunned as he had by his own father and brother. They had been a team, and he'd been squeezed out.

He'd had a choice: to curl up into a ball, to fade away or to make them notice him. He'd chosen the latter. When he was sixteen, he'd begged his father to send him to the right racing academies, and his persistence eventually paid off. Luckily, he was talented, and when his father didn't give him a position on the De Rossi F3 racing team, he was quickly snapped up by another team. It didn't take him long before he'd made his way to F1, joined another racing team, and when the press questioned why he wasn't on the family team, his father smoothly replied that he didn't believe in nepotism. Taz had to earn his spot on the De Rossi team. It couldn't have been further from the truth. His father hadn't wanted him on the team full stop.

That had only fuelled the fire of his ambition. While driving for a rival team, he became a top driver, a contender and Alex's rival. Then Ben was killed at Imola, and his father, hampered by his words about only employing the best, reluctantly offered Taz a place next to Alex. He nearly refused, but the De Rossi team was the pinnacle of racing. And like his father, he never settled for second best.

Nothing about their family dynamics changed, and he kept his distance, never reacting to his father's and brother's gaslighting, understanding that they needed to find a chink in his armour to exploit. He became…stoic. Unimpressed. Unemotional.

Appearing impassive and detached became a habit, and eventually, after years of training, he became the way he acted.

Until tonight when he kissed Millie. Maybe it had started on Thursday when he realised she could see past his cold façade to the storm brewing under his layer of ice. Or maybe it started weeks ago when he'd first looked into her purple-blue eyes and felt himself tumbling.

Bottom line, he'd boxed himself into a corner. He didn't like the way she made him feel, and his first impulse, and the easiest option, was to be shot of her. But if he demoted her back to being his press liaison officer, he'd still have to work with her, which defeated the objective. And he didn't have any cause to fire her. Either action would make him look like indecisive.

Besides, firing Millie a day after promoting her would also be grossly unfair. He'd raised her expectations by telling her she was promoted, and ripping the opportunity away would be a cheap shot. Or was he grabbing onto any excuse to keep her around? He shoved the idea away, uncomfortable with its many implications. He'd promoted her: He would stick by his decision and make it work. And pray that in the morning, everything would be back under control.

CHAPTER FOUR

LATER THE NEXT MORNING, Millie walked into the penthouse suite of the team's hotel, her eyes widening as she took in the skyline views of the Pudong district, Shanghai's Bund and Huangpu River, and the Oriental Pearl Tower from Taz's high-in-the-sky hotel suite. It wasn't just the views outside, it was the suite itself too, the luxurious furniture, the baby grand piano and the bank of floor-to-ceiling windows. The white, black and grey colour scheme was interrupted by splashes of tangerine. The décor was stark, hard, severe…just like her boss.

Talking of, where was he? He'd been discharged from the hospital earlier this morning, and he knew she was here to see him. The only place he could be was the suite's bedroom. After their kiss last night, she wasn't going anywhere near where he slept, so she dropped her bag onto the couch and walked over to the telescope standing in the corner of the room.

She'd lain awake for most of the night, her thoughts bouncing around her brain. Ben's death, Taz's kiss, how she viewed herself, how her parents viewed her. Why she was here, how she was going to save Taz's reputation, if that was even possible. Why had he kissed her? Promoted her? What did it all mean? And why was life getting *more* complicated, not less?

'Millie.'

Millie turned, and Taz stepped into the room to her right. Behind him, she saw a brief glimpse of a massive free-standing bed in the middle of a huge room. But it was Taz's appearance that caught her off guard. He was a stylish dresser and usually favoured designer suits with open-neck shirts and expensive shoes, or business casual outfits that screamed *style and sophistication*. Today he wore a loose T-shirt over straight-legged track pants, his big feet bare. His hair was unbrushed and his scruff was thicker than before. He looked disreputable and danger-ous and so, so sexy.

She dropped her head and cleared her throat, cursing her attraction. Maybe it was because he was the polar opposite of the men she'd dated over the past few years. They'd been bland, uninspiring and so very uninterest-ing, all the things her parents accused her of being. When she finally took time to work out why she sat through the interminable meals and boring weekends, why she toler-ated bad or mediocre sex, she realised it was because she believed she didn't deserve any better. Tired of wasting her time, she'd distanced herself from men completely.

Sabotaging herself had to stop, and she decided she needed to find a new way to navigate life, to figure out how to view herself going forward. That was why she'd upended her life to join the F1 circus, to take on a new challenge. And if part of her life lesson was dealing with her attraction to this charismatic man, then so be it.

Had life thrown Taz into her path to challenge her habit of second-guessing herself?

Millie cleared her throat and nodded to his cast. 'How are you feeling?' she asked, sitting on one of the two bucket chairs opposite the enormous boxy couch.

'Like they shoved a pin into my finger to stabilise the bone,' he retorted. Sarcastic as always. Millie watched him, but nothing in his eyes or his expression suggested he was going to mention what had transpired between them last night.

He was back to being her grumpy, detached, frequently annoying boss. This was what she wanted, right? For them to go back to normal, and Taz being sarcastic and difficult was normal.

Taz dragged his free hand down his face. 'Sorry.'

Damn, just when the earth had stopped moving under her feet. Taz apologising was *not* common, but Millie didn't know how to handle him doing it, so she ignored his snappy, one-word apology.

'Being indisposed makes me tetchy. Showering was a bitch, dressing wasn't easy. I've been in a foul mood all morning,' he added.

She could imagine his frustration at only having one working hand. Millie waved her phone at him. 'I got your message to meet you here, and here I am. Can we talk about you promoting me now?'

He frowned at her. 'Why is that such an issue? Most people would have thanked me a thousand times over by now.'

God, he was arrogant.

'Because I'm not sure I want the promotion, and more importantly, I don't know if I can do it!' she half shouted, surprised she'd raised her voice. She'd trained herself not to react emotionally. In her family, it wasn't safe to lose her grip on her emotions, to let them see that what they said bothered her. It only made it worse. Why was she losing that tight grip now? What was it about Taz that pushed her to the limit?

He brushed her words aside with the swipe of his hand, unfazed by her reaction. 'Of course you can.'

His conviction was contagious, and for a few seconds, she believed him. Then reality strolled back in, and she shook her head. 'You don't understand. I haven't worked on a big campaign.'

'It's the same principle, isn't it? To build and maintain a positive image, right?'

Essentially. 'Well, yes, at the most basic level,' she admitted.

Taz's shrug suggested their discussion was over. But she still had questions. 'I don't think—'

'It's done. Moving on.' Just like that.

'The F1 stewards doled out community service as a punishment for me pushing the rookie,' he informed her, sitting down on the couch and casually placing his bare feet on the glass coffee table. He looked at her and grimaced. 'In a meeting late last night, they agreed that I'd punished myself enough by punching the wall and putting myself out of commission, but they still had to censure me.'

Millie had to think fast to keep up with him. She'd come back to her promotion and her worries around it later. 'Community service isn't so bad,' she said, linking her hands around her knee. 'How much do you have to do and by when?'

'The only proviso was that I had to make an impact, so it's up to me.'

Millie mentally ran through some options. 'You could do what your brother did and visit a children's hospital or an orphanage, speak at high schools, do a shift at a community kitchen feeding the homeless.'

An emotion she couldn't pinpoint flickered in his eyes before they turned flat and unreadable. Was it frustration, annoyance or anguish? She wasn't sure. 'No. I don't want to be seen to be taking the easy way out by doing what he did,' he replied. But something in his tone suggested it was a pat answer, one he trotted out to get over what he thought was a bump in the conversation.

'Your brother got a lot of good press doing those appearances,' Millie pointed out. But doing community work had reportedly been part of Alex's personality, fed by his deep desire to help people less fortunate than himself. Alex was as lauded as much for his philanthropic endeavours as he was for his racing. Losing him was a tragedy. It must still be deeply painful for Taz.

Yet, how could two brothers grow up in the same house, under, as she believed, the same set of circumstances and turn out so different? She'd often wondered if she'd had a sibling whether they would have been like her, quiet and withdrawn, or more like her parents, a sunflower constantly turning its head to the light, happy to bloom?

Ben was raised in much the same way as her, but he'd been happier, sunnier, more confident. Was it a male thing or was it because he discovered his passion for racing young and was able to pour all his energies into his sport? The sport that he lived—and died—for.

'Why do the good ones always die young?' she murmured.

'You assume Alex was good?' Taz asked, dropping his feet and leaning forward, his eyes blazing with an emotion she couldn't identify. Millie frowned, confounded by his fierce expression. In reality, she'd been thinking about Ben but wasn't about to reveal that. She rarely told anyone about her semi-famous parents, and she'd yet to tell anyone, including Taz, that she was related to Ben, partly because talking about him was still hard and partly because she wanted to avoid comparisons between her and her gregarious and popular cousin.

Still, his reaction was...confusing to say the least. Almost as if he was daring her to contradict the narrative.

'Um...he was well-known for giving his time and attention to causes he cared for, always visiting sick kids in the hospital or making guest appearances to help charities,' Millie stated, confused.

'He was a saint.' Taz's tone was so bland she wasn't sure if he was being sarcastic or not. Then as quickly as it had come up, he moved on.

'I haven't had a moment to read Mika's reports on the PR my crash and fracas caused. Update me.'

'It's a train wreck,' she warned him.

'Not unexpected,' Taz murmured. 'Give it to me straight.'

Millie took a deep breath and told him how he was being called *temperamental* and an *uncontrollable, spoilt, overprivileged hothead.* How he was risking his title and his brand, and when was he going to grow up?

'That reporter I wanted you to meet on Thursday? She's now one of your harshest critics. Her podcast, the one where she discusses how different you are to Alex, has shot up the popularity charts.'

Taz narrowed his eyes at her. 'If you tell me I shouldn't have blown her off on Thursday, I will fire you.'

Chance would be a fine thing. Millie gritted her teeth. She'd almost let that phrase slip. She could handle managing his press—press releases, interviews, the usual chaos—but being responsible for his *image*? Spinning it, rehabilitating it? That terrified her. Taz didn't need a PR manager, he required a miracle worker. Someone with the nerves of a pro gambler and the skills of an acrobat juggling ten balls on a unicycle. Someone who exuded confidence, who could command the narrative with unquestioned charm.

How could she possibly reshape his image when she barely understood her own? Sure, she could write a flawless press release or schedule his interviews down to the second. But transforming the world's perception of him? That required unshakeable confidence and bold, unapologetic chutzpah—qualities she didn't possess.

'Why isn't your PR team here?' she demanded, still looking for an out and hating herself for not throwing herself into this new challenge like she knew she should after all the promises she'd made to herself and Ben. 'They have far more experience than me.'

'They are also set in their ways and have a narrow way of thinking,' Taz replied. 'Why are you still trying to talk yourself out of this promotion?'

'Because you need someone more qualified!'

'We're done talking about this, Millie,' Taz retorted. 'You're bright, observant and clear-thinking. Stop putting yourself down, and get on board.'

Millie's mouth opened and closed in shock. It was an

unexpected compliment, and she didn't know how to respond to it.

'Tell me about the press coverage.'

His sharp order made her pull her thoughts together. 'You're getting annihilated. And the sponsors aren't happy.'

'Because any impact on my brand is an impact on theirs. And if they are complaining, then I'm in bigger trouble than I thought.'

His main sponsors were an energy drink company whose advertising was risqué and always controversial and a worldwide travel company whose tag line was that *If it wasn't naughty, it wasn't nice.*

'It's a perfect storm,' Millie admitted. 'People aren't happy you went on a date with Meredith—'

'That's not what happened, and you know it.'

'The truth doesn't matter, perception does. After the press implied you are sleeping with your brother's fiancée,' Millie countered, 'you crashed, putting your championship in jeopardy. Then you pushed a rookie driver, one of the nicest around, and you punched a wall, putting yourself out of commission. The press and public hate unforced errors, Taz.'

'I don't need you to rehash my mistakes,' he said, black ice frosting his voice and eyes. 'And regret doesn't change a damn thing.' He raked his hands through his hair and linked his fingers behind his neck. 'I need to move forward, and that requires solutions and strategies, and I need them *right now.*'

A discreet knock on the door interrupted their conversation, and Millie let out a long, unsteady breath, grateful for the reprieve. She might see herself as underqualified, acutely inexperienced, but for some inexplicable reason Taz seemed to believe she could cope with the pressure. He was putting his faith, and more importantly his reputation, in her hands.

He was Taz De Rossi, famous for hiring the best and firing them when they didn't live up to his exceedingly high expectations, but... She rubbed her hands over her face.

But if he believed in her, perhaps it was time she stopped doubting her capabilities. At the very least, she owed it to herself, and to Ben, to try.

Taz greeted the room service waiter and walked over to the floor-to-ceiling window. The waiter poured coffee and left, as quiet on exit as he was on his entrance.

Millie joined Taz at the window, handed him a cup of black coffee and folded her arms. 'So I've been thinking...'

'Is that dangerous?' he asked, but Millie caught the delicious, but very unexpected, glimmer of amusement in his eyes. So Taz had a dry sense of humour. Good to know.

'Look, I think you're unwise to promote me, but it's obvious that you need to rehabilitate your reputation.'

'I am *not* doing hospital visits or visiting youth groups.'

'If you did, you would be compared to Alex,' Millie mused. 'The public would accuse you of being inauthentic, of trying to ride the coat-tails of your brother's sterling reputation to restore yours. It would be a disaster.'

His expression hardened, and Millie wondered if she'd hurt his feelings. No, that wasn't possible. Nobody was sure Taz *had* feelings. Though his kiss last night suggested otherwise. *Don't think about how his mouth felt on yours, Millie...*

'Please, don't hold back,' Taz murmured.

Sarcasm, or not? She didn't have time to try and figure it, or him, out. Millie put down her cup and paced the area in front of the window, flicking her thumbnail against her front tooth, thinking hard.

'Apart from racing, what do you do well?' she asked. Before he could speak, she answered her question. 'According to the internet, you are a fantastic skier, a better polo player and a golfer with a plus-one handicap. It's been said that if you didn't go into driving, you could've made a living in pro polo or golf.'

Millie couldn't see Taz doing either: Both were far too tame for a man who lived life at a thousand miles per hour. And drove cars at a third of that speed.

He collected wine and owned a holding company that owned and operated the De Rossi team and its many subsidiaries. He had a vineyard in France and a villa in Tuscany. A brownstone in New York—not the same one where his brother died—and a flat in London. No doubt he had an English country house too. Then it hit her.

'I have an idea...'

'Should I be scared?'

Millie narrowed her eyes at him. Please, the man didn't *do* scared. 'Why don't you do what you do best?' she asked.

He lifted his cast. 'Because my hand is out of action,' he replied at his mocking best.

'You're a *socialite*, an A-list celeb, someone who is as at home at parties and functions as you are on the track. We can use that to rehab your rep.'

Taz closed his eyes. 'I haven't even heard your proposal yet, and I know I'm going to hate it.' He sighed and gestured for her to continue.

'I think you should offer yourself as a drawcard, for charities to raise money from your presence at their functions. We can contact charities and ask them how they could use you. Maybe it's to co-host a ball, be the VIP guest at a cocktail party, attend a golf tournament or offer meet-and-greet sessions. It would qualify as community service, and it'll help rehab your appalling reputation.'

'I'm no Boy Scout, but I don't quite have a foot in hell,' he protested.

Millie started ticking off points on her fingers. 'You and Phoebe have had a tumultuous on-off relationship for years—'

'I think calling it a *relationship* is stretching the truth,' Taz interjected.

'Noted. You're rude, impatient and, frankly, uncontrollable.'

'Who is supposed to be in control of me?' he shot back. 'I own my team, I call the shots, I make every decision.'

Good point. 'You never push back on bad publicity.'

He shrugged. 'People can write what they like, believe what they want.'

So confident. 'Up until this point your saving grace, from a PR point of view, has been your exemplary behaviour on and off the track. Journalists have often commended you for not carrying your bad-boy antics onto the track and into your professional life... Until now,' she concluded.

He tensed, and Millie knew she'd made her point. 'They—the press and the fans—are asking whether your personal life has spilt over into your professional life. People might excuse your antics off the track, but they won't stand for it on it.'

He nodded. Was he taking her comments on board? 'You're not offended?' she asked.

'I'd much rather be hurt by the truth than comforted with a lie,' Taz replied, lifting his shoulders in a quick shrug. 'So you think lending my pulling power to charities will redeem me?'

'Along with an apology to the rookie? Yes. Well, it certainly won't hurt.'

'I intended to make my apology to him in private. I think it means more that way.'

Millie agreed. 'A public statement is also necessary, Taz. A photo of the two of you shaking hands would be even better.' He was unlikely to agree, but what was the worst he could say? No?

'I wanted to catch him before he left for the two-week break before Miami, but,' he said as he held up his cast, 'the operation delayed me.'

Throughout the F1 season, everything the team needed at a race—from invaluable cars and the team's headquarters to tyres, fuel and Taz's preferred brand of coffee— was transported to every location the sport visited around the world. Their next stop would be Florida, for the Miami Grand Prix. Formula One was one big moving circus: Set things up, race, take them down. Rinse and repeat.

'Can you apologise to the rookie by video call? That way we can get a statement out to the press quicker.'

Taz didn't look happy at the suggestion but finally nodded. Millie did a mental fist pump and, because her luck was holding, pushed for more. 'And will you consider collaborating with charities?'

His eyes connected with hers, and Millie felt the pop of a champagne cork in her stomach, the fizz of bubbles. 'Draw up a list of twenty charities, a mixture of established and new, and let them make a one-page pitch or short video message as to how best they could use me. I'll decide who to support.'

Excellent. That was a solid win. Except there was one little fly in the ointment. Phoebe. Who tended to resurface in Taz's life whenever there was an excellent promo opportunity. She couldn't let their turbulent relationship spoil his PR rehabilitation. 'I can explain you meeting Meredith, as she was Alex's fiancée. But Phoebe is a troublemaker, and she has to stay away from this, Taz.'

The woman in her, the one who'd kissed Taz last night, would prefer Phoebe to drop out of Taz's life entirely. Millie told her to be quiet. She wasn't allowed an opinion.

His eyebrow lifted at the use of his first name, but she didn't break eye contact. He needed to know how deadly serious she was on this point. Millie gathered her courage. 'Her reputation is worse than yours, and the charities don't deserve to be caught up in any drama. If she's going to be around, then tell me and I'll find another way to rehab your rep.'

'I like your idea,' Taz replied, his agreement shocking her. 'And Phoebe and I are done. Permanently.'

Really? Millie hoped Phoebe had got that message. 'I track the press releases mentioning your name, and she's been giving interviews left and right, saying that you'll be back together soon. That you will be heading to the Caribbean to recoup and reset your relationship.'

He scoffed. 'There is *nothing* to reset. I made it clear to her a few days ago, before I left London, that we are over.'

He sounded like he meant it, but Phoebe was a bad penny who kept showing up. But Millie saw the warning light in his eyes and decided to heed his silent admonition. The subject was closed.

She looked down at her iPad, reflecting that she'd made more progress than she'd expected.

It was time to go. 'I'll get working on the press statement and researching charities.'

'Link the charities to where we are racing next. A Miami charity for Miami, an Italian charity for Imola.' Millie swallowed. She'd been trying to forget they were heading to the racetrack where Ben lost his life. She didn't know if she could do it. But the Imola race was still a month away, and she'd worry about the emotional impact of being at the crash site later. She had bigger problems right now.

'I'll see what I can do.'

She stood and picked up her bag and pulled it over her shoulder. She shouldn't ask but she couldn't help herself. 'Are you going back to London or New York?'

'Not that it's got anything to do with you, but I'm not sure yet.'

Just when she'd thought he might be evolving into a halfway decent conversationalist and boss, he'd proved her wrong—yet again. The memory of their kiss still lingered, but she was determined to be professional and courteous.

Taz was a master at being difficult. He was also exceptionally good at testing her patience. *Deep breath, Millie.*

'Have a good flight. I hope your recovery goes well.'

She smiled, and when he didn't say anything she turned her back to him and walked to the hallway and the front door of his palatial suite.

'Millie…'

She slowly turned. He sat on the arm of the couch, and she could feel the intensity of his stare. 'That kiss…'

She thought they'd dodged that landmine, that his silence on the subject was his way of telling her that it meant nothing. Heat crept up her face. She had no idea what to say or what he wanted from her, so she hugged her iPad to her chest as a bead of sweat ran down her spine.

He kept looking at her, and it took all her willpower to keep her from bolting out of the door. When the tension became too much, the silence too weighty, she spoke. 'I work for you, *Mr De Rossi*. What happened was against company rules.'

'I know. It's *my* company. But it was a truly excellent kiss.'

She wanted to grab his shirt and shake him, not that she'd be able to make his muscular frame budge an inch. This man, she was convinced, was born to drive her mad. 'I think you enjoyed it as much as I did,' he stated, his tone silky and deliberately provocative. Was he trying to get a rise out of her?

Be sensible, Millie. Do not let him goad you into being reckless or admitting to your attraction. 'I don't get involved with people I work for, Mr De Rossi. It would be highly unprofessional. Besides, you have a girlfriend, and she would scratch my eyes out if she found out.'

'I thought I explained that Phoebe is no longer in my life. I dislike repeating myself.' Should she ask whether he was certain Phoebe had received the message? No.

He'd already clocked her interest; she didn't need him to know that he *fascinated* her.

Millie lifted her chin and gathered her courage. 'Apart from not dating bosses, I don't date bad boys. I don't date *at all*.' Well, not anymore.

'Pity,' Taz drawled.

Millie gripped the door-handle and twisted it with more force than necessary. She needed to get away from Taz before she did something really stupid. Like dropping her possessions and walking into his arms. Hauling that T-shirt up his chest, kissing his neck...

Leading him into his bedroom. She shook her head at her lust-coated thoughts, not recognising herself. She wasn't a lose-her-clothes, roll-around-the-bed-with-a-billionaire woman.

Besides, there was too much at stake for her to risk making such a mistake. Taz had the power, wealth and influence to recover from his mistakes...

But she did not.

CHAPTER FIVE

Miami

IT WAS A beautiful spring day in Florida, hot and blue, and when the stewardess opened the jet's door, a stream of hot air rushed into the air-conditioned plane. Taz unclipped his seat belt and stretched, wishing he'd slept for more than a few hours last night.

He shouldn't have accepted an invitation to meet some friends at Lily's last night. But after reports started surfacing that he was hiding away because he couldn't handle criticism and was sulking, social media influencers started echoing the nonsense. Millie sent him a message telling him to get out and about and to look cheerful while doing it. He'd thought about ignoring her directive—he wasn't the kind of man who let anyone, least of all inconsequential voices online, dictate how he lived. He did what he wanted when he wanted. Always had. But then he remembered how hard Millie was working—some of her emails were time-stamped after midnight her time—to salvage his tarnished reputation. He rubbed the back of his neck, slightly concerned, and feeling a little guilty that he might've handed her a poisoned chalice.

After Shanghai, he'd needed to retreat, to nurse his

self-inflicted wounds, to mentally beat himself up in private. He'd put everything he and his team had been working for in jeopardy and had torpedoed his personal, private goal of being a better racer than Alex, the only competition he could win against his dead, seemingly perfect brother.

But the longer he was alone, the louder whispers of past failures, the brutal echoes of his father's harsh words and Alex's casual dismissal of his talent became. Sometimes solitude wasn't peace, and sometimes the only way to evade the past was to drown it in bars and clubs, pumping with too-loud music and shouted conversations.

So he'd gone to Lily's in London, and naturally he'd run into the press.

And Phoebe, who'd tried to renegotiate her way back into his bed. He'd sharply and succinctly shut her down. He'd told her when they first started sleeping together that he didn't make long-term connections, but she thought she could change his mind and that she would, eventually, take his name.

Not happening. Besides, being a De Rossi wasn't as marvellous as the world thought it was.

All his life, he'd been looked at through the Alex lens and been found lacking. As a result, he'd gone out of his way to be as different from his brother as he could be. And if you were always acting, then how could anyone get to know the real you? Any personal connections were false because nobody knew him.

On the surface, he had everything anyone could want: the houses, the money, the cars, the clothes…but no one to share them with. And that was how he liked it. He'd been his mum's kid, and after her death, neither his father nor his brother knew how to, or wanted to, handle a grieving child. They'd pushed him away, and he'd spent the rest of his childhood and teens desperately trying to catch up, to reach the ever-increasing bar they set for him. His only hope of beating his brother at anything was on the racetrack. Once he won his fourth championship, the world would have to admit that he was a better driver than Alex. In their eyes he'd never be as good a man. He'd never taint the De Rossi brand by telling the world who Alex really was, but he'd revel in being known as the better driver.

But he'd put that in jeopardy by losing his temper in Shanghai. He'd apologised and approved a short press statement publicly apologising to the rookie, the FIA and his fans. Millie's statement made him sound authentic without being obsequious. She'd also talked him into a press conference in—he glanced at his watch—an hour. The first since his crash and where he'd announce his community service plans and put forward the charities he'd be supporting.

He should be practising, talking, *breathing* cars. But he was now sitting on the sidelines.

Taz pulled his aviator sunglasses onto his face and jogged down the plane's steps to the waiting SUV. The driver opened the door, and he pulled back on seeing Millie sitting in the far corner, her face pale. She wore a brightly coloured patterned sleeveless sundress that hugged her curves. Her hair, as usual, was piled up on her head, and she'd smudged her eyeliner and mascara. She looked…beautiful.

And therein lay his other problem. For the last two weeks, he hadn't been able to stop thinking about their kiss, wishing that it had lasted longer, that he'd pushed for more. Her mouth had been sweet, her hair soft. Her perfume was light, and her fingers on his jaw and her hands on his body had felt so damn right.

He rubbed his hand over his jaw, thinking that recently Millie had come into proper focus for him. Oh, he'd been attracted to her from the moment he met her—he was a sucker for the combination of blue eyes and reddish-gold hair—but because of that and because she worked for him, he'd thrown up more shields than he usually did.

With Millie, lust and work collided, and it was as frustrating as hell. He wanted her, and that night, after one of the worst days in a long, long time, he'd lowered his control and given in to the temptation of kissing her. It had been better than he'd imagined, and he had a damn good imagination. He shook his head at his wayward thoughts as he climbed into the car. She worked for him and was off-limits.

'Millie? I didn't expect to see you here,' he said, shutting the door. He wondered when last she'd had a decent night's sleep. She looked…stressed. 'Everything okay?'

'Oh, I'm peachy,' she muttered. She glared at him. 'Could you not have stayed out of trouble for a couple of weeks, Taz?'

He was a grown man, someone who owned and operated a racing team and all its subsidiaries, a company worth billions. Nobody told him what to do or how to act. Especially someone whose salary he covered. Despite that, he enjoyed her annoyance, liked the way it pushed colour into her cheeks and the light of battle in her eyes. He knew she preferred negotiating to arguing, so he admired her attempt to venture out of her comfort zone.

'Lie low, I said. It wasn't that big an ask!'

Right, she'd run out of rope.

'Check your tone, Millie,' he suggested, keeping his voice low. He raised the privacy screen between them and the driver. 'Would you like to tell me—*calmly*—why you are angry?'

'You went to Lily's last night.' She pushed her iPad into his hands.

He didn't bother to look down. 'So?'

'The bad press was finally beginning to die down, but your partying at Lily's last night has the press once again questioning your sincerity. There are over a dozen stories today, all insinuating that you aren't sorry, that having a good time is more important to you than racing and that you're not taking your career seriously.'

Racing was the only thing that meant anything to him. Taz ran his hand through his hair, his back teeth grinding. He wanted to justify his actions, something he never did. 'You told me to go out!'

'I meant for you to go for coffee or visit a friend! I did not say that you should go to Gossip Central!'

He struggled to hold on to his temper, knowing he wouldn't bother if this was anyone other than Millie. What was it about this woman that had him checking his words and reining in his temper? Why her? And why, for God's sake, now?

'I got to Lily's shortly after eleven. I'd been working, and I couldn't sleep. So I went out. I went into the VIP section where I had two whiskies and then left.'

'Phoebe was there.'

Taz clenched his uninjured hand.

'She's quoted as saying that you've lost your interest

in racing and that you have a temper. And she's seen you lose it. She tossed gas on the already-fiery press reports.'

Taz gripped the bridge of his nose and closed his eyes. He could *not* catch a break. After last night's hopefully final last rejection, he could see Phoebe lashing out. But insinuating he'd lost his temper with her? That was low.

Would this drama ever end? And why did he feel so unbalanced? Was it because he wanted Millie to believe he was better than he was portrayed? And why was he worried about what she thought?

She was nothing like his usual women; she was grounded and down to earth. Impatient with nonsense. He liked her. More than he liked most people. But this conversation proved that she, like everyone else, couldn't see him clearly. Perhaps her astute observation back in China that there was nothing between him and Meredith had been a fluke.

He felt irrationally disappointed.

'Look, I know it's nonsense, but the world doesn't.'

Her words doused the fire under his temper, and a measure of calm returned.

'I'll admit I'm impatient when things don't go my way or when my orders are not followed. But I have never, ever lost my temper with a woman.' He never cared enough to expend that amount of energy. He nodded at her iPad, resentful at having to explain. 'I ended it, permanently, at the beginning of the season. She's now stirring the pot, unhappy because I rejected her again last night.'

'She wants you back?'

He lifted one shoulder and shrugged. 'Phoebe doesn't take no for an answer. Last night's *no* was final and emphatic. She understood that, was angry and wanted her revenge.' Last night he couldn't help comparing Phoebe to Millie, and the ex-model came up very short. How? He didn't know. He couldn't define his attraction to Millie, but it didn't make it less potent.

'By calling tabloid journalists at midnight?'

Calling? He smiled at her naïveté. 'She just needed to walk outside the club, a bunch of them were outside. They shouted questions at me, but I ignored them. They would've asked her about me, and angry because I rejected her, she probably vented to them.'

Millie looked out of the window as they travelled down the highway to the purpose-built temporary circuit around the Hard Rock Stadium in Miami Gardens.

'I've never worked for anyone standing in such a bright spotlight,' she murmured. She looked at him, and he caught the confusion in her eyes. 'Being your press liaison officer was easy, but this is a high-profile campaign.'

Great, now he was a campaign. 'Maybe you should hire someone with more experience,' she said, biting her sexy bottom lip.

This again? How many more times would he have to explain? 'Millie, I could hire anyone I wanted, the best PR company in the world. I do not want them, I want *you*.'

He couldn't move past the thought that no one would do a better job than her. It was a gut reaction, and his intuition had yet to steer him wrong.

Their eyes clashed and held, and awareness slid into all her purple-blue gaze. Intuition and work aside, did she know how much he craved her? In his bed, under him, in the most primal way possible. Her curly hair spread over his pillow, hearing her pants as he pleasured her, lathing her pale skin with his tongue, tracing the contours of her curves with his teeth. Her eyes widened, and she touched her top lip with the tip of her tongue, a wholly subconscious reaction. He was experienced enough to know she was as attracted to him as he was to her, but she needed to make sense of what she was feeling.

Lust was lust, a basic diving force. It didn't have to mean anything. A clash of pheromones and chemistry, it frequently didn't. There was no need to make it more than it was. But Millie, he suspected, was someone who dissected it from every angle, to make sense of what she was feeling. Her brain would make her body-related decisions. And that meant he wouldn't see her naked anytime soon.

Dammit.

He shoved away his lusty thoughts and told himself to concentrate on business. He'd promoted her because she saw *him*, not the owner or the driver but the man he was, more clearly than anyone had before. That was worth *everything*.

'You were my press liaison officer and now you're my PR person,' he told her, getting back to the subject. 'I expect you to do your job.'

She released a long sigh. Millie chose her battles, which suited him fine. He didn't like people arguing with him; he preferred they did it his way the first time he asked. 'It would be helpful if your ex would stop stirring the pot,' she muttered. 'Would you consider—'

No. There was no chance he'd ask Phoebe to shut up. He wasn't going to open a shut door. 'People will think what they think, and I don't care. I only care what they think about my team and my racing, my abilities as a driver. Everything else is superfluous.'

Focusing on his racing was how he managed to stumble through those years after Alex's death and then his father's. Sorting through the legalities and establishing his right to the De Rossi assets had taken some time and a chunk of money. His dad's will stated that Alex was to inherit *everything*, and because he hadn't made a new will yet in anticipation of his marriage, Alex had left everything to him. If had Alex had died after their father's death, it would've been a simple process, but it happened the other way around. It took the hiring of expensive lawyers to establish he was the rightful heir to the De Rossi assets. Knowing Matteo hadn't wanted him to have even the smallest slice of the De Rossi empire had been, and still was, acid in an open wound.

When he won a fourth championship, the world would see him as successful in his own right. It was, after all, something neither his father nor his brother had managed to achieve. He'd be seen as himself, and not a reflection of his brother and father. It would be *his* achievement, untainted by the old resentments and harsh memories.

He'd vowed to himself that this season would be drama-free. He'd all but stopped bar-hopping and partying, and it was bad luck that on two of the few occasions he'd been out at clubs, he'd met up with Meredith and Phoebe. Did the gods of good PR have it in for him?

'Tell me about the charities you've short-listed for me to support,' he asked, placing his ankle on his knee. Millie ran through the charities and gave a brief explanation of what they did. Within ten minutes, they'd decided on him lending his support to five organisations: attending a polo cross tournament this weekend, a golf tournament, a ball, a garden party and a cocktail party. Five charities over six weeks.

Millie tapped her pen against her lips, lips he desperately wanted to kiss. 'It's a pity you don't have a decent, nice girlfriend, someone who can accompany you to these events.'

'I've been doing solo events for years now,' he pointed out.

'But a pretty girl in a pretty dress, someone who isn't known for getting into arguments and being confrontational, would be helpful.' She nodded at his phone. 'Do you know any women like that?'

It was true that he preferred women who were a little edgy.

Millie was anything but edgy. But something about her called to him, and if the chemistry crackling between them translated to the sheets, sex would be explosive.

She works for you, De Rossi. That would be a stupid move.

'Well?' Right, she'd asked him a question. What was it again? Did he know any nice women? Of course he did: the wives or girlfriends of fellow drivers, and his senior staff. It was true, men liked to party with bad girls, but they invariably married good girls. Not that marriage was something he'd consider. The De Rossi brand was his wife and mistress and took up all his time. And best of all, it didn't talk back or act out. And he didn't have to consider its feelings or opinions.

'I know *you*.'

Their eyes collided, but Millie waved his words away. 'Anyone else but me? Anyone you can ask to be your plus-one?'

As the person responsible for rehabilitating his image, she was going to be accompanying him everywhere he went for the next six weeks anyway. Why deal with the hassle of having to make nice with someone else when she could do the job? '*You* can be my date.'

She stared at him, then laughed. 'Yeah, right,' she scoffed.

Annoyance spiked. Was she denigrating him or herself? Both rankled. 'And why not?'

'Firstly, because I am the last woman in the world you would date,' she told him. 'I'm not your *type*.'

There was a note of desperation in her voice, tinged by resignation. And she wasn't being coy.

'But you are, on the surface, nice and normal, and you are pretty,' he countered, using her words against her.

She frowned. '*On the surface?* What does that mean?'

He narrowed his eyes, intrigued by the glimpse of deeper layers beneath the surface. She had secrets, and he wanted to know what they were. Surprising, since he normally never cared. Neither could he tell her that when he got her naked, he simply knew she'd turn wild in his arms. He chose to ignore her question, knowing she wasn't ready to hear what he wanted to do to her in bed.

You have enough problems without adding bedding Millie to the long list, De Rossi. Get your head in the game.

'You are going to be everywhere I am,' he stated. 'It would be far easier if you acted as my date.' If he asked anyone else to be his date, there'd be complications, expectations he wasn't willing to meet. He'd have to entertain her beyond the events and navigate a minefield of raised hopes and assumptions. But Millie? Millie was easy. As long as he kept everything surface-level—and he would—she could play the role of his date, then slip back into her role as his PR person when the event was over. No drama, no fuss, no strings.

Having Millie as his date wasn't just convenient, it was safe. Predictable. And Taz needed a little predictable. And some easy. 'Millie, it makes sense.'

'To you, maybe,' Millie retorted. 'I stay in the background, Taz. It's what I do. I don't make headlines, I *spin* them. I couldn't think of anything worse than standing in the limelight next to you.'

Her words made a sharper cut than expected, and he mentally flinched. He knew too well how it felt to stand in someone else's shadow. He'd spent a lifetime trying— and failing—to be worthy of his father's praise, and as much time coming to terms with the con job Alex had pulled on the world.

Or maybe somewhere deep inside him, in those places he rarely visited and never acknowledged, he wanted her or someone like her to be proud to stand next to him, proud to be with him, to think that the sun and moon rose with him.

Not because he was Taz De Rossi, Formula One driver and team owner, not for the fame and wealth that came as effortlessly as some of his track wins. But for the man he wanted to be. The man beneath the façade.

But it was senseless, and pointless, to think that way, and he wasn't a stupid man. The world didn't work that way. It ran on transactions, and he was a brilliant negotiator. 'How much?' he bluntly asked.

'How much for what?' she asked, confused.

He snapped his fingers, impatient. 'For you to act as my girlfriend,' he clarified.

'You're offering to *pay* me to date you?'

Why not? He had an obscene amount of money and could afford it. And she was right, having a sensible girlfriend would look good as he stepped into his temporary role as a brand ambassador, as someone there to attract interest in the charity.

'If I invited someone else, I'd have to pay for her flights, her hotel room, her food and probably her clothes. I'm already paying those costs for you. You'd need clothes, cocktail dresses and some ball gowns, some designer outfits… Stop frowning, I'll pay for the clothes you'd wear while acting as my date.'

'I'm not going to *be* your date!' Millie's voice rose as they turned into the business entrance to the track.

'Five hundred thousand pounds.'

Her mouth dropped open, and she shook her head. 'Seven fifty?' he offered. He could carry on inching his way upwards. He was still in petty cash territory.

Millie stared out the window, her shoulders up to her ears and her cheeks cherry red. 'It was your idea,' he pointed out.

'I never thought *I* would be the star of the show,' she shot back.

'You won't be,' he told her, fighting his amusement. 'That's my job. You would be there to provide a little additional sensible sparkle.'

'You're off your head,' Millie told him as the car pulled to a stop in front of the area allocated to the De Rossi entourage.

Maybe. 'Well, it's you or nobody,' he told her, reaching for the door-handle. He'd learned how to negotiate when he was a kid with his taciturn, ungenerous father, and he'd honed his skills since then. Everyone had a number, and he'd find Millie's. Florida heat and humidity rolled into the car. 'Seven hundred and fifty thousand pounds for acting as my girlfriend at five events isn't a bad deal, Millie.'

'I think your Shanghai crash addled your brain,' Millie told him, shoving her iPad and phone into her enormous tote bag.

'Is that a *yes*?' he asked, looking back at her from outside the car.

She pushed her hand through her wayward curls. 'It's an *I'll think about it*.'

Taz swallowed his grin, knowing he had her. Nobody *thought* about such a big offer. She'd say yes because it would be the easiest money she'd ever make. And the best he'd ever spend.

Because Millie, for some reason that eluded him, was the only person he could see himself spending any time with. She was smart, down to earth and surprisingly sassy.

But she was also dangerous.

He hauled in a deep breath, reminding himself that he was Taz De Rossi and that he could easily resist her. He'd walked away from princesses and principal dancers, actors and models without a backward glance, and he wouldn't allow himself to fall under the spell of his down to earth press officer.

And even on the off-chance he did, he was an F1 driver, the best around, and he regularly danced with danger. He knew exactly how to exit any situation unscathed.

CHAPTER SIX

THE DRIVER PULLED into the parking area close to the entrance for VIP passes and pulled to a stop, letting the car idle. Millie gathered her possessions along with her thoughts and prepared to exit the car. Three-quarters of a million pounds? Had she heard him correctly? Just for acting as his girlfriend? That was…

Madness. He was joking…right?

Instead of climbing out of his side of the vehicle, which was on the right side of the entrance, Taz followed her out of her door, took her laptop bag out of her hand and slung it over his shoulder. She heard the roar of the fans gathered outside as they recognised Taz.

Millie looked over to the crowds and the waiting press, cameras in hand. She tipped her head in their direction. 'You've got fans watching you and cameras pointed your way. Try to smile.'

She wanted to discuss his wild offer, but there were too many ears around, too many eyes on them. When she was next alone with him, she'd sit and explain why she couldn't do it, why that wasn't possible.

There were seven hundred and fifty thousand reasons why it could be possible. The money aside—*she could do-*

nate it to the trust she'd set up in Ben's name—*why wasn't it possible?* And why did the voice asking sound like Ben?

You crashed out of my life. You don't have an opinion anymore, she crossly told him.

You keep saying you want to figure out who you are, where you fit...

I don't fit in, Ben.

Millie scrunched up her nose and shuffled on her feet. That was what she told herself when Ben invited her to join him at Monaco or Silverstone. Not fitting in and knowing how to handle their rich world was also how her parents justified leaving her alone when they jetted off on holidays to places like Monte Carlo and Ibiza, Jamaica and Rio.

That was then, this is now. How do you know if you don't fit if you don't try?

What if I embarrass him?

Dead Ben actually scoffed. *Taz isn't easily embarrassed, and do you think he'd ask you if that was a concern? When it comes to women, Taz is a picky bastard.*

And yes, her ego just doubled at the idea of playing Taz's girlfriend. Millie placed a hand on her jittery stomach and reminded herself of what was important. She was trying to figure out who she was and where she was going, how she was going to navigate the rest of her life, but she wouldn't be able to do that standing on the sidelines. Taz was offering her a way to step into Ben's world, her parents' world.

Of all the ways she imagined coming to terms with her past, with Ben's death, with her parents and her lack of confidence, she never thought she'd be acting as Taz's girlfriend when she did it. Her parents had practiced smiles and knew how to stand, when to answer press questions and when to appear mysterious. Taz played by a different set of rules, mostly because he was rich and powerful enough to make them up as he went along. But she was just an ordinary woman living an ordinary life; she wasn't rich, famous, important or charismatic. She far preferred to stay away from the lenses of any cameras, to live a quiet life.

If she took Taz up on his offer, she'd be thrust into the spotlight and would have the eyes of the world on her. She was, as she'd been told a million times, not cut out to stand in the limelight. She wasn't even sure she was cut out to do PR. Sometimes her insecurities, fed by a lifetime of her parents' criticism, threatened to overwhelm her.

Also, accepting his offer was tantamount to inviting her family back into her life. They would barrel back in, blithely ignoring the past and their inattention and neglect. They'd insert themselves into her life, playing at being one big happy family, all the while desperately hoping her relationship with Taz would raise their own public profile. Her parents were publicity parasites.

No, she couldn't risk that happening…

Millie frowned, annoyed by her reaction. Why was she allowing her parents to influence her decision? Wasn't she trying to break that habit? Taz was offering her a way to explore whether the messages she received and believed as a child and teenager, that she wasn't good enough or that she was an embarrassment and didn't fit in, were true. If she managed to navigate the wealthy, sophisticated world that Taz was so comfortable in, she could rewrite the criticisms she'd been fed and swallowed. Believed. And if her parents swooped in? What would she do then?

Millie released a long breath, feeling overwhelmed. She could cross that bridge if and when it came to that. First, she needed to decide whether posing as Taz's girlfriend was something she wanted to do.

It was a lot of money to turn down. With three-quarters of a million, she could make a difference in many people's lives and do it in Ben's name. How could she pass that opportunity up? She couldn't, could she?

But this wasn't the time to make rash decisions. She'd consider his offer later; right now she needed to work. She hurried to catch up with Taz's long-legged stride to the entrance to the track. 'Your press conference will take place in the press room shortly. The journalists will quiz you on your actions in Shanghai and will have questions about your injuries. And I can carry my laptop bag.'

'I've got it, and you sent me an email briefing me about today's press conference. It's fine.'

She braked, not sure she'd heard him correctly. She'd expected him to moan and complain about sitting down for a Q and A. 'Right, good.' She squinted at him. 'Did you hear what I said?'

He gave her a quick eye-roll. 'I'm not deaf. And if we don't keep moving, we are going to be swarmed.'

Fans and members of the press corps started drifting in their direction, and Millie started to walk, battling to keep up with Taz's pace. The noise level intensified as they approached the crowd that stood between them and the turnstiles that would allow them access to the paddock. Millie glanced up at Taz, whose sunglasses covered his startling eyes. A fan asked him to pose for a photograph, and Taz—notorious for ploughing his way through crowds—stopped to take the selfie, then another one. What was happening here? Then, to make things even stranger, he grabbed her hand and threaded his fingers through hers.

She tried to tug her hand away: He was going to give everyone the wrong impression, and that was a headache neither of them needed. If he'd let go of her hand, she could slip behind the crowd, swipe her pass and wait on the other side of the paddock.

A journalist pointed his camera at their linked hands. 'Are you in a relationship with your press liaison officer, Taz?' he demanded, his eyebrows raised.

Taz looked down at their hands but didn't release the clasp. 'You know I never answer questions about my personal relationships.'

Millie tugged her hand out of his, and when he looked at her, she motioned to the turnstile. 'I need my hand to get my pass out of my bag,' she hissed.

Taz pushed his sunglasses into his hair and caught the eye of one of the security guards manning the turnstiles. 'Can you let us through, Juan?'

The turnstiles clicked open, and Millie stumbled into the paddock, still feeling the heat of Taz's palm on hers. She watched as he casually pushed his hands into the pockets of his pants, and she caught the corners of his mouth lifting.

'You did that on purpose!' she shout-whispered, as they walked to the De Rossi section of the paddock.

Taz greeted a driver and shook hands with another. After answering a question about his hand from another team owner, he looked down at Millie. 'I didn't want to lose you in the crowd,' he told her.

What nonsense! There weren't that many people on

this side of the fence, and she could've easily dodged them if he'd let her go. No, he was trying to manipulate her into acting as his girlfriend and thought by creating the perception, she'd bend.

It was something her parents would do, had done. Like Taz, they never took no for an answer. 'I won't be pressurised into acting as your girlfriend, Tazio De Rossi' she told him, surprised at her vehemence. And, maybe, a little proud of herself. It was about time she was able to stick up for herself.

He stopped, pulled her out of the way and folded his arms. 'What do you have to lose?' he asked, keeping his voice low, intimate, a hint of a challenge in it. 'You're going to be spending the next six weeks with me anyway. Why not get an extra million for holding my hand and looking at me in a somewhat adoring manner?'

He'd increased his offer again. The mind boggled at what he was offering, thinking of all the things she could do with that kind of money, like how she could fund Ben's dream of training talented underprivileged teen racers. But she needed to keep thinking clearly. 'Everyone will think I am unprofessional mixing business and pleasure,' Millie shot back.

'Everyone knows I am difficult to work with. They are already impressed you've stuck it out this long,' Taz responded wryly. 'Most of my press liaison officers barely last the week, never mind two months. They certainly don't get promoted.'

He wasn't wrong that this could help people see he wasn't the man they thought he was. She was also trying to step out of her comfort zone, to do things that challenged her, be less like her ultra-cautious self. *You're mad if you don't take him up on his offer, squirt.*

Ben's voice was so clear, she could swear that if she turned she would see him standing there.

Be brave, take a chance.

She stomped her foot and released a low hiss of frustration. She had Ben's voice in her ear, and if she said no, she felt she'd be letting him, as well as herself, down.

'Is that a *yes*?' Taz asked.

Millie scowled at him. 'A million. A third now, a third in three weeks, the balance at the end of six weeks.'

Taz dared to grin at her. The blasted man never doubted the outcome of his proposal. What was it like being so certain all the time, so convinced that the dominoes of life would fall in line for you?

'Deal.'

Millie thrust her hand at him, expecting him to shake it and was caught off guard when Taz clasped her fingers and lifted them to his lips. She shivered, and ribbons of heat and light darted down her fingers and up her arm. Damn the man for being so sexy, and relentlessly charming. 'Excellent.'

He wrapped his uninjured hand around hers and tugged her toward the De Rossi section of the paddock. 'I'm expecting a decent turnout for the press conference,' Millie said.

'I'm Taz De Rossi, and they've been baying for one. They'll be there,' Taz stated with complete conviction. 'They wouldn't miss it.'

Oh, to be so self-assured. But he was right, as they'd been flooding her email and phone requesting interviews or asking for a comment. 'I have a draft statement I'm still working on. I'll get it to you within thirty minutes,' she told him, very conscious of her hand in his. People started noticing, their eyes darting to their linked hands and their eyebrows rising. Five minutes in and she already felt like a goldfish in a too-small bowl.

'I'll look at it, but expect changes,' Taz stated, pushing her ahead of him as they walked into the area allocated to the De Rossi Racing team. Of course he would change what she wrote, because Taz never did what was expected of him. Millie watched as members of his technical team approached him.

Taz squeezed her hand before letting it go. 'Text me when you've finished with my statement, and we can go over it. If I'm not in the pit, find me.'

Millie nodded and watched him walk away, surrounded by his people, everyone wanting something from him. She'd been swept up into Taz's world, into the maelstrom he created. He was taking her acceptance to be his fake girlfriend as a given.

And she was, probably, going to let him.

And if she found herself floundering in choppy, unfamiliar waters, she had no one to blame but herself.

Taz, sitting alone at the long table, a raft of microphones in front of him, tapped his finger on the white linen tablecloth and schooled his expression into what he hoped would pass for pleasantness. He was a pro at press conferences; they were a necessary evil, but there were better ways to spend his time.

Taz sneaked a look at his watch and sighed. They were running ten minutes late, mostly because members of the press were still trying to get into the now-packed room.

Millie stood in the corner to the right of him, her iPad clutched, as it frequently was, to her chest.

Unfazed by the eyes on him, he saw Millie staring at a spot on the floor, the corner of her lip caught between her teeth. Her shoulders were an inch from her ears, and he knew she was second-guessing herself and him. He lounged in his chair, wearing his usual mask of detachment, pretending to scroll through his phone.

He had a girlfriend. He grimaced at the childish term; it didn't suit him, a man who'd spent his life avoiding emotional entanglements. His career was his greatest love, the only mistress he ever needed. He was doing this to benefit his company, to bolster his brand. Dating Millie was a strategic move to repair his image, to keep his fans, sponsors and the media focused on what mattered: his path to his fourth championship. After a few weeks, everything would go back to normal. Or whatever passed for normal in his world.

Tension crawled up his spine, and he told himself to relax. This wasn't a big deal. But it was, because this was Millie. The same Millie he kept imagining naked beneath him—or on top of him because, honestly, he wasn't picky—her skin flushed with pleasure, her breathless moans in his ear.

He wanted Millie almost as much as he wanted that fourth consecutive championship. A sliver of self-doubt slid under his skin. What had he gotten himself into? And why did the thought of being with her thrill him? Racing was his world. Winning his satisfaction. Yet here he was, his thoughts on a woman he employed. A woman he was paying an obscene amount of money to hold his hand and play a part.

Maybe if he banged his head against the table hard enough, he'd knock some sense into himself. But then again, maybe not.

'Ladies and gentlemen, Taz De Rossi will now read a statement, after which we will take a set number of questions.'

Right, he was up. After pushing his hand through his hair, he looked down at the statement Millie had carefully prepared. *Off his game, irritable, the rookie should've slowed down while navigating the corner. The strain of driving and owning a team had caught up with him…*

It was a raft of excuses for his questionable behaviour, and he knew the press corps would lap it up. It was also all BS. He picked up the statement and scrunched it into a ball. Noticing the surprise on the faces of the journalists directly in front of him, he almost smiled.

'I could sit here and give you a dozen excuses about my behaviour in Shanghai, tell you how stressed I am, how the demands of owning a team and being its number one driver got to me last Saturday. I could tell you that…' He looked at Millie amused by her shocked expression. But was that horror or approval he saw in her eyes? A mixture of both? 'But I'm not going to. The truth is that I lost focus on that race, my mind wasn't completely on my driving. Jackson did nothing wrong, the blame for what happened in Shanghai should be placed on me.'

Oh, well, he'd stepped into the hurricane, so he might as well see if he could ride his way out of it.

'I have apologised to Jackson personally. I'd also like to apologise to the sponsors and my fans.' He lifted his cast-covered arm. 'I am paying for my stupidity, as I should.'

The silence in the room was absolute, and all he could

hear was the scratching of pens on paper and the occasional cough from a reporter at the back of the room. The rebel in him enjoyed their shocked silence.

'You know I was given the punishment of community service by the FIA stewards,' he said. Should he mention Alex's philanthropic efforts? No, he was not going to invite them to make comparisons between his brother and himself. They would do that anyway, without his help. And, as always, he'd probably come up short.

'I intend to complete that service by working with five charities until my injuries are healed, hoping to shine a spotlight on what they do.' He went on to name the charities, giving a brief description of the organisations' work. 'You can find links to all the charities on the De Rossi website, and if you can, please donate. Any amount is helpful and would be gratefully received.'

'I will be at all the races, supporting my team and, hopefully, not driving them too crazy.'

That statement elicited a laugh. 'I'll take a few questions now.'

A wave of questions rolled over him as the journalists shouted over each other.

He glanced over at Millie, and she gave him an encouraging smile. Surprisingly, it instantly dropped his irritation levels. Strange, because no one ever made him feel like that before.

'Can you tell us how you felt when Jackson nudged you in Shanghai?'

God give him strength. This? Again? 'As I've said, twice now, my behaviour was unacceptable. I'm not going to rehash it again.' He couldn't keep the annoyance out of his voice.

How much longer was he supposed to endure this? He glanced at his watch. He'd give them a few more minutes, and then he'd leave.

'Are you worried about losing championship points?'

Of course he was; he wasn't an idiot. If his nearest rival won all the races he'd miss, they'd be level on the board. It made him furious to think that he'd wasted that lead because he'd lost his temper. That he was the disappointment his father believed him to be. Had called him such to his face on numerous occasions.

Thinking back, he preferred his father insulting him than ignoring him: At least he could be bothered to interact with him. But those stretches when he was consistently disregarded or dismissed were worse. They were right. Bad attention was better than no attention at all. Being made to feel insignificant and unimportant was far more dangerous to the psyche than being told you were bad.

In his father's eyes, the world's eyes, Alex had been as perfect as a human could be. Handsome, intelligent, charming, nice…he had it all so Matteo hadn't hedged his bets or spread his attention. Everything he wanted in a son he had in Alex.

'You seemed quite chummy with your press liaison. Something happening between you?'

It took Taz a moment to make sense of the question. When he did, he leaned back in his chair and placed his hands on his thighs, his fingertips digging into the fabric of his pants. He made sure his expression remained unruffled. 'You know I never answer questions about my personal life.'

'Is Phoebe still on the scene?' the reporter persisted. 'Are you going to the Caribbean with her?'

Damn, the urge to launch himself across the table and punch the smirking journalist was strong. But he hauled in a breath—he'd done enough damage lately. This line of questioning grated more than usual. Normally he shrugged such queries off and gave them no more thought.

It was because the journalist had mentioned Millie. His instinct to protect her left him reeling. When she appeared with him at the polo tournament on Saturday, she would be on everyone's radar, something he wanted, *needed* if he was going to ride out this media storm. The press would focus on them and would blow the smallest interaction into a drama. It was part of dating a celebrity, of being seen with him.

Taz pushed a hand into his hair. What would it be like to have someone standing in his corner, providing support for no extraneous reason?

He brushed his thoughts away. He wouldn't know what to do with a serious girlfriend—or how to handle her. It wasn't for him, never had been. Trust wasn't something he could do on a long-term basis.

Millie was different—interesting and funny—but she was his employee and would be playing a part while she handled his PR. This was a business deal.

And because it was business, he had to stop thinking of her as a potential lover, someone he wanted in his bed. He was aware of the power imbalance: He held it all, and he had to tread carefully through this minefield. Had to play the game, get this deception underway—and draw on every bit of his willpower to keep his hands to himself.

'Taz? *Taz?*'

He jerked, his attention returning to the curious faces in front of him. He turned up his cuffs, pushed back his hair again and cleared his throat 'I didn't hear your question. Would you mind repeating it?' he asked, thinking that he was being a great deal more polite than he wanted to be.

'Are you and Phoebe still on track for that Caribbean getaway?'

He let out a slow breath, and turned toward Millie, pulling up a smile he hoped was both affectionate and intimate. His gaze locked onto hers, and he caught the flicker of panic she couldn't quite hide.

Better to rip the bandage off. Brutal, clean. Yes, this was an ambush, but this way he could take control of the narrative. Control was everything. Besides, it was time for her to start earning her million pounds.

'Ladies and gentlemen,' he began, keeping his tone smooth, 'allow me to introduce Millie James. Not only does she manage my PR, but she's also my significant other.' He let that land, enjoying the shocked gasps followed by stunned silence. 'Our relationship is still new, but we both agree it holds a lot of promise.'

The crowd in front of him gaped, and he handed them a wry smile. 'I'd ask you to respect our privacy, but let's be honest—that's not going to happen, is it?'

He rose to his feet, the scrape of the chair on the floor the only sound in the room. Then, taking his time, keeping it casual, he crossed the room to Millie. He cupped her cheek with one hand and brushed his mouth over hers—keeping the kiss soft, but deliberately possessive. He swallowed her shocked gasp, and her fingers trembled as he laced their fingers together.

'Let's go,' he murmured against her ear before pulling her toward the exit. The room behind them erupted with shouted questions, some laughter and the general chaos that followed the detonation of a conversational landmine. He didn't care.

As always, he'd accomplished exactly what he'd set out to do.

CHAPTER SEVEN

LATER THAT NIGHT, Millie left the second bedroom in the hotel suite—apparently sharing a suite was part of the devil's deal she'd agreed to—and crossed the lounge area to the streamlined galley kitchen, hoping to find some hot chocolate. If she could find whisky, she'd add a slug, hoping the liquor would help her get a few hours of sleep.

She'd been prepared to return to her own hotel room, but Taz had other ideas. When he'd ordered her to move into his suite, she'd protested—loudly and quite vehemently—but he wouldn't budge.

'Are you looking to give the press a story?' he'd demanded. 'The world expects us to share a suite. *I* expect us to share the suite.'

He ended their discussion by calling an intern to arrange the collection of her belongings and move them to this suite twenty floors up.

This was the first time she'd shared a living space with a man, and Millie would've felt uncomfortable with a non-celebrity, someone normal. Sharing a fantastically expensive suite with Taz, incredibly famous and ridiculously good-looking, felt surreal.

How was she supposed to handle this? Handle him?

Dressed in loose and comfortable pink-striped pyjamas, she heated some milk and tried to loosen the tension in her shoulders and neck.

It had been a long day, and she'd have a longer one tomorrow…or was that later today? Either way, she had a raft of meetings, including an appointment with the stylist Taz kept on retainer. He was flying in from New York courtesy of Taz's private jet, with a vast range of clothes, shoes and accessories in her size. She and Taz had agreed that, while she was on the track, she'd stick to black jeans, her high-tops and De Rossi–branded shirts, but when she accompanied Taz to his charity appearances, she needed to look like someone he'd date.

Sophisticated, cool, at ease.

Everything she was not.

Millie dashed a shot of expensive whisky into her drink and walked back into the lounge area, dropping to sit on a too-low backless couch in front of the floor-to-ceiling windows. The lights of Miami spread out before her, and she wished she could head down to South Beach, take in the Art Deco buildings, and experience some street food.

As Taz's press liaison, she'd been able to fade into the background, slipping around the press coterie with nobody noticing. But as Taz De Rossi's *girlfriend*—his brand new, unexpected and highly scrutinised girlfriend—she couldn't take a step without having a press pack on her heels. They were a bunch of hyenas, looking for an angle, hoping for a soundbite as they shoved microphones in her face. They made her feel disoriented and exposed.

She'd seen the pictures from the press conference earlier, which were now online, and she barely recognised herself. Wide-eyed and pale, she looked like a terrified deer frozen in the headlights of a sixteen-wheeler truck. Young. Vulnerable. Out of her depth.

Being with Taz wasn't for the faint-hearted. But she wasn't a child anymore, and if she was going to survive this, she had to find some courage and learn how to play the game. And she didn't have any time to waste.

Taz's reputation and a million pounds were at stake...

It was so much money. While he was alive, Ben quietly sponsored up-and-coming racers, and after his death Millie had established a charity in his name to continue that tradition. After the courts had told Ben's parents that she was his legitimate heir, Millie moved the many millions she inherited from Ben to the charity's account. Eight or so years later, she still got a kick knowing there were drivers on the F3 circuit who wouldn't be there had the charity not stepped in to help. Ben, she knew, would approve. After all, it had been his dream. She'd also inherited his London flat and a car, so she didn't need the money that Taz was paying her. She planned to donate that to Ben's charity as well.

It seemed the right thing to do.

And for a million pounds she could and would fake confidence, channel sophistication and play the part of Taz's perfect girlfriend.

But with publicity came the risk of her parents sliding back into her life to take advantage of her and her newly acquired fame. How long would it take for her parents to hear about her dating Taz? Not long, she decided. They'd quickly find a way to leverage her connection to Taz. What form would that take? Would they fly into Miami? Start dropping his name everywhere they went? Sell their story to a tabloid on the flimsiest of pretexts? When it came to her parents, truth never stood in the way of good publicity. That was part of the reason she'd stayed away all these years. She didn't want that life. It had damaged her already.

A part of her wanted to call it quits, to retreat, but then she'd lose the chance to find herself in this world that Ben had been such a huge part of.

And wasn't she done, or trying to be done, with allowing her parents to influence how she lived her life? Millie heard the snick of an opening door. She turned, sucking in a sharp breath when she saw Taz step into the lounge, nude but for the cast of his wrist and a pair of black sleeping shorts.

His chest was incredible—broad, lightly dusted with dark hair, and tapering to a stomach showcasing his defined six-pack. Every inch of him, from his thickly muscled shoulders to his strong, sinewy arms and long, sculpted legs, screamed raw, masculine power. He was, quite frankly, a work of art wrapped in impossibly tempting packaging.

Her mouth went dry looking at him, so she took a hurried sip of her hot chocolate, hoping it might restore a little moisture and distract her from the bedroom-based thoughts racing through her mind.

The expensive whisky made her catch her breath, and she spluttered.

'Millie?' he asked, in a rough-with-sleep voice. 'It's after two. What are you doing up?'

She lifted her cup. 'I couldn't sleep so I made myself something to drink. I hope you don't mind.'

He ran a hand through his messy hair. 'That's fine.'

She grimaced. 'I also helped myself to what I think is

very good whisky. Whisky that isn't meant to be added to hot chocolate.'

He walked over to her, taking the mug from her hands. He sipped and grimaced. 'I'll have a whisky without the hot chocolate.'

'Want me to get it for you?' she asked. They might both be in their sleepwear, but she did work for him.

'I've got it.'

Millie tried not to react when Taz sat next to her, heat rolling off his body. She thought about asking him to put on a T-shirt, but then he'd know she'd noticed his body. No, it was better to keep her eyes on the lights of this amazing city spread out in front of them.

'Are you in pain?' she asked, wondering why he was awake.

Out of the corner of her eye, she saw his shoulder lift and fall. 'It's more annoying than uncomfortable.'

'Why can't you sleep?' he asked, lifting the heavy crystal tumbler to his lips.

It was her turn to shrug. 'I've got a lot on my mind.' She was still trying to wrap her head around everything that had happened today.

'Maybe we should talk about how we are going to act when we are together at these charity events,' she said, placing her mug on the floor at her feet. Along with backless couches, the decorators responsible for these expensive suites didn't like side tables either.

Sometimes less was less. And impractical.

'I'm not a fan of standing in the spotlight. I don't enjoy having eyes on me,' Millie said, biting the inside of her cheek.

Taz leaned back on his elbows and looked at her. It took

all her willpower to keep her eyes on his gorgeous face and not take a lazy stroll down his fantastic body. *He's your boss, Millie. Half-dressed boss and a short-term fake boyfriend, but you can't forget that he is your boss.*

'How do you think we should act, Millie?'

She didn't know. That was why she was asking him. She threw her hands up in the air. 'Are you going to hold my hand, put your arm around me…?' She wanted to ask him whether he'd kiss her too, but her tongue wouldn't form the words.

He looked at his glass, frowning when he saw it was empty. Grateful for the reprieve, Millie snatched it from his hand, walked over to the small bar and poured him another two-fingered shot. 'Should you be drinking this with painkillers?' she asked him, handing it over. Their fingers brushed and electricity erupted on her skin. Dammit. With everything else that was happening in her life, why did she have to be so attracted to the man as well?

'Well?'

She frowned at Taz. 'Well, what?'

'How do you know what standing in the spotlight feels like? Are you an influencer or the aristocratic daughter of an earl? The girlfriend of someone famous?'

'Ha, no. As if.' But he wasn't too far from the bull's-eye. Should she tell him who her parents were? It hadn't occurred to her before, but perhaps he deserved to know who he was getting involved with.

He leaned forward, rested his arms on his thighs and dangled his hand holding his glass between his legs. 'How do you *know*?'

He wasn't going to drop the subject. If nothing else, she should tell him about Ben, before he found out via someone else. Secrets were difficult to keep in any work-place. 'I'm the daughter and niece of pretty famous ac-tors.' She gave him their stage names and recited some of their popular roles.

Taz frowned, his razor-sharp mind making connec-tions. 'I met them, years ago. Through Ben Brennan.'

It didn't take long for him to connect the dots to Ben. Would the final piece slot into place? His gaze sharpened. 'You're related to Ben, aren't you?'

'He was my cousin and, in many ways, my protector and my best friend growing up.' Millie sighed. 'Our par-ents, both sets, love attention. If there's a camera, they want to be in the shot. I was dragged to art galleries and show openings and premières and made to pose. I never could, not in the flattering way they wanted me to, and the photos with me in them always bombed. They even-tually decided it was easier to leave me and Ben at home with our nanny. My mum and his mother are twins and share *everything*.'

'That sounds ominous.'

He had no idea. 'Ben and I had four parents, all equally demanding, equally narcissistic, equally uninterested in anything but themselves. Ben and I became a team to keep them at bay.'

'Sounds like a nightmare,' he commented. 'But why keep your connection to Ben under wraps?'

A good question. How to explain? She stared at the floor. 'Ben asked me, probably every week, to come see him race, but I was in my late teens and early twenties when his career took off, and I wasn't particularly inter-ested in cars.' She saw him wince and smiled. 'I found every excuse to dodge a visit.'

'Why? It's such a dynamic, exciting place.'

It was one thing to feel insecure and another to admit it. She looked away, looking for the answer in the view. He, surprisingly, didn't push her for an answer. 'Ben was, genuinely, one of the best people I knew. I was gutted by what happened to him,' Taz said, sounding sincere. 'Was he the reason you joined De Rossi Racing as a press officer?'

Taz could be, occasionally, incredibly perceptive. And there was something about the way he looked right now. Less like a racing team owner or arrogant driver and just like a man who made her feel that she could open up to him.

'Next month will be the tenth anniversary of Ben's death. I don't expect you to understand, but I joined this world, his world, as a tribute to him.' And as a means to find, within herself, the confidant, secure woman Ben believed her to be. 'But it's turned out to be more complicated than I expected,' she added, linking her hands around her knee.

'Because of me?' He was quiet for a few seconds. 'Are you wanting to bail on being my fake girlfriend?'

'Yes. But I can't.'

'Because of the money,' he stated, his voice flat and his expression unreadable.

She nodded. 'Yes, because of the money. I can't afford to pass up the opportunity to raise a million quid for his charity. It would normally take us years to raise so much money.'

'You're donating the money I'm paying you to a *charity*?'

It was wonderful to see him caught off guard for a

change. 'I would *never* fake- or real-date you, or anyone, for personal gain,' Millie told him.

'I think you'd better explain,' Taz told her, his voice brusque.

Millie quickly told him about her inheritance from Ben and about the charity she'd established in his name. Taz kept his eyes on her face, his expression stoic, but she knew he was taking in every word. At the end of her two-minute-long ramble, he nodded but didn't comment.

Millie hated herself for wanting his praise. She shook off her disappointment and pushed back her shoulders. 'Coming back to my original question… How are we going to act when we are out and about?'

He looked at her, his expression still serious. 'How do you want me to act, Millie? It's your call.'

'I don't know. That's why I asked.'

He took her hand and linked his fingers in hers, his thumb stroking the top of her hand. 'We'll have to hold hands.'

When his hand swallowed hers, she felt grounded and safe. But the action itself was innocuous, so she nodded. Taz moved closer, his thigh against hers, and dropped his head to lay his lips on her temple. 'A couple of light kisses?'

Another nod, and her eyes went to his lips, soft in contrast to his heavy stubble. His face came closer, as his hand ran down her shoulder to her hand and back up again. He swiped his lips across hers, in a kiss that was as hot as it was brief.

'That's as far as I will go,' he told her. 'In public. And in public is where our bargain ends.'

She frowned, suddenly confused. 'You've lost me,' she admitted.

'I'm paying you to act as my girlfriend, but everything that happens privately has nothing to do with our bargain,' he told her, his voice harsh.

'What's going to happen privately?' she asked, her heart stuttering when he smiled.

'God, you're sweet. And a little naive.'

He wasn't mocking her. He seemed in awe of her. He brushed the pad of his thumb over her lower lip and leaned in close so that his words brushed her lips. 'In private, I'm going to seduce the hell out of you, Millie.'

Taz looked into her lovely face, his thumb still on her lips. He should get off this couch and go back to his room, but there was more chance of an asteroid striking this penthouse suite. He wanted Millie. It was as simple and as complicated as that. And he always got what he wanted.

And now that he knew where his million pounds would land, a massive barrier to seducing her had crashed and shattered. He wasn't paying *her* but a charity. And yes, she was still his employee, but he now felt the pendulum of power had swung back to the middle, levelling the playing field. If they kept work and play separate, if they played by the rules—*his rules*—they could explore their intense attraction.

But the rules had to be explained. There was no room for misunderstandings.

'Millie, I want you, I'm not going to deny that. I would love to take you to my bed, strip you down and make you mine.' Her eyes widened, as he'd expected them to. She clearly wasn't used to men being direct, telling her what they wanted and how they wanted it. But being direct was the only way he knew how to be. 'I can't wait to have you under me. I want to be inside you, giving you the best orgasm of your life.'

It wasn't a boast; he knew he was an exceptional lover. He made it a point of being good at everything, and a long time ago he'd decided that if a woman was gracious enough to let him love her, then he was obligated to make her see not only stars but also a meteor shower or two.

'But what we do when we are naked has no bearing on you being my fake girlfriend, the money I am paying you or your work as my press or PR person. When the world goes away, you and I are equals, and there's no power imbalance in bed.' There was zero fun in coercion. 'Nothing you do or say will have any bearing on what happens in the outside world.'

He saw her swallow. 'I want to take you to bed. But you should know that all we'll ever be is lovers. I don't fall in love. I *won't* fall in love. I'm not interested in a relationship or commitment. The only thing that's important to me is my team and winning a fourth championship.'

Millie touched her top lip with the tip of her tongue, and he wished she wouldn't. He was already steel-hard, and when she made those unconsciously sexy actions, it took all he had not to lay her back against the cushions and ravage her mouth, slowly making his way down her body.

'Uh…'

Great, he'd rendered her mute. He lifted his eyebrows and waited for her to gather her thoughts. But instead of speaking or retreating, she surprised him by sliding her cool hand around the back of his neck and lifting her mouth, a silent invitation to kiss her.

Taz obliged. Her lips on his were soft and feminine, and when his tongue slipped between her teeth, he tasted chocolate and whisky. And Millie. His tongue swirled lazily around hers.

'This isn't like me,' she murmured, as she pulled away and moved onto her knees, trying to get closer to him, and lust, hot and electric, shot down his spine and straight to his groin.

He lifted his mouth from hers to respond. 'It is when you're with me. I need you to touch me, Millie. *Everywhere.*'

His words, as he intended them to, granted her permission to explore, to stop thinking and start doing. Who'd made her question herself, made her so skittish? Her small hands raced over his shoulders and down his back, and she slid her finger under the elasticised waistband of his shorts while she moved the other hand to cup his butt. As he suspected, beneath her layers of doubt was a sexy, sensuous woman. He responded by dialling up their kiss, turning it hotter, *raunchier.*

Fuelled by her impatience, his hand moved from her hip and moved up and under her pyjama top, massaging her breasts, his fingers exploring her already-tight nipples. She straddled his thighs, the inside of her knees pushing into his hips and she scooted forward, rocking herself into him. Through their clothes, her hot core connected with his erection, and need raced across her face.

Impatience roared through him, chased by desire, so he lifted Millie off him, laid her on her back and quickly stripped her sexy pyjamas off her lovely body. Taz groaned when he slid his hand between her legs, bathing his fingers with her arousal.

He lifted his eyes and looked into hers, and his heart—dammit—missed a beat. Her gaze was surprisingly fierce. 'I know I'm naked, but I'm not ready to have sex with you.' Her words landed, and he struggled to make sense of them.

Shit... He blinked, trying to slow down and think. 'Okay.'

He immediately removed his hand, and she whimpered, obviously disappointed. 'I know, I'm sorry. I just can't...not yet.' She bit down on her bottom lip and looked away. Her lovely chest rose and fell as she hauled in some air. 'But I don't want to stop either... So can you touch me, Taz? And I-I'—God, even her stutter was adorable—'and I can touch you. If you want that.'

He did. Hell, he'd take anything she could give him right now. He held her eyes and saw the anxiety in them; it seemed she was bracing herself for his anger. He wasn't cross: She had the right to change her mind, to set the boundaries. He lifted his hand to stroke her cheek, needing to banish her worry. There was no place for it between two naked people. 'Okay, let's do this instead.'

He lay on his back and lifted her onto him so that her heat landed on his shaft, her knees on either side of his thighs. Her slick heat enveloped him, and he dug his fingertips into her hips, urging her to ride him. She quickly picked up the rhythm, and soon they were panting, both seeking that exquisite release. A part of Taz couldn't comprehend that he was so turned-on by something that was—if he were being honest—not much more than heavy petting. But he was close, so close...

So was she. The city lights danced on her skin, and in the seductive light he took in her flushed face. But he needed to see all of her so, using his core muscles, he half sat up and latched his mouth on her nipple and pulled it up to the roof of his mouth. She was so hot, so responsive…so into him and what they were doing.

And he, the master of control, someone who knew how to delay gratification, was going to come, hard and very soon. Shoving his good hand between them, he found her clit and told her to wrap her hand around him. She fisted him and rolled her hand to the top and he felt the pressure build at the base of his spine.

'Millie, are you going to come for me?' he growled, not recognising the need and desperation in his voice. A part of him wanted to pull back to regain some much-needed control, but the finish line was just a few seconds away.

As his words hit her lips, she started to shake. Her eyes closed, her mouth fell open, and she screamed her satisfaction. Ridiculously, stunningly turned-on, unable to help himself, he let himself go.

He felt like she'd gripped his soul and squeezed. Taz closed his eyes, trying to get his breathing back under control. Millie moved off him, and he watched through half-closed lids, his heart a loud bass drum in his ears, as she picked up her pyjamas. Then she crossed the lounge and slipped, still naked, into the second and smaller of the two bedrooms.

The snick of her lock was as loud as a pistol shot.

The next morning, after a couple of hours of restless sleep, Millie paced in front of the bedroom window, her bare feet sinking into the plush carpet as she tried to make sense of her too-fast thoughts, her heart thumping at the raunchy memories from last night. She rested her forearm over her eyes, as heat rolled through her and her heart bounced off her ribs.

She couldn't even argue that she'd been seduced or that she'd...*slipped* into the situation. No, she'd tumbled into it, head first, heart racing, with no thought for the consequences. Taz's heated gaze and growled compliments hadn't helped her keep her wits about her. She'd been lost the second she saw the raw appreciation in his eyes—how he watched her, and how he reacted to her touch and her kiss.

Can't think about that now. She *worked* for the man and was *pretending* to be his girlfriend. Millie banged her fist against the window. Her life was veering wildly off-track. She hadn't come here to entangle herself with Formula One's most notorious playboy. She'd joined the De Rossi team to remember Ben and to reconcile who she was with who she wanted to be. But instead of doing some intense self-reflection, instead of figuring out if she could be brave or feel more secure and self-assured, she'd fallen under Taz's seductive spell.

If he was still alive, Ben would argue that kissing Taz—and what followed—had been an act of bravery, a leap far beyond her carefully guarded comfort zone. But that wasn't the kind of courage Millie was searching for. She wanted to change her life, to become someone she respected, not someone who let her control unravel the moment a hot man turned his devastating eyes on her and told her he wanted to take her to bed.

And yet...*last night*. God, she'd wanted to burn. She'd loved his intensity, that laser-focused passion, directed solely at her. And yes, it had been everything she'd imag-ined and more. A firestorm. A revelation. Hot and sexy and indescribably intense. And it had only been a taster. Taz making love to her might kill her.

She shook her head, before resting her forehead on the window. It couldn't happen again. It *wouldn't* hap-pen again.

Yes, they'd agreed to this ridiculous fake-dating ar-rangement, but that was as far as it went. They weren't lovers, and they certainly weren't friends with benefits. From this moment forward, they would be professional. Polite. They had to ignore their crackling chemistry.

Because no matter how much her body begged for more, Millie refused to let herself become another Taz De Rossi pit stop. How could she go from dating boring men to being celibate for years to sleeping with the world's sexiest driver? That didn't make any sense, it wasn't a straight line, and she needed to backtrack. Immediately.

She couldn't think of Taz as anything more than her boss, her fake boyfriend. She couldn't forget the hard les-sons she'd learned as a child and young adult: the closer people got to her, the more pain they could inflict. Her parents were supposed to love her, but they didn't. She and Ben were supposed to grow old together, but he'd died. It was far easier to distance herself from men, from people, thus avoiding the possibility of being emotion-ally eviscerated.

But she'd never reacted to a man so quickly or so strongly as she had to Taz, so that meant she had to pull on her emotional running shoes and put a lot of distance between them. Fast.

Decision made, Millie whipped around to find her

laptop, to check the schedule. They needed to be at the charity function this afternoon around three and she remembered that Taz wanted to spend some time in the pit with his technical staff. Her next task was scanning the papers and online publications for reactions to his press conference. She was expecting them to be good, but with the press you never knew.

She started a list on her phone and headed for the suite's lounge. She typed as she walked and hit a hard, bare chest. She gasped and slapped her free hand on Taz's muscled pec. It was so hard, so hot, and it was only then that she took in that he was only wearing long loose silk pyjama bottoms.

Taz curled his hand around her neck and covered her lips with his, his tongue sliding past her teeth to tangle with hers. She sighed and sank into the kiss, and it took her a few seconds, maybe a minute, for her brain to remind her that kissing him wasn't something she was supposed to do.

She was being paid to act as his girlfriend, even if it was for Ben's charity, and if she started sleeping with him…what did that make her? No! No! *No!* He'd explained, very directly, that what they did together clothed, naked or at any stage in between—was between them, and wasn't part of their deal. She couldn't start entertaining those denigrating thoughts. It wasn't fair on her. Or on him.

But damn, kissing him, being with him, was such fun. And being on the receiving end of his sexual skill was as addictive as a Class A drug.

It took all Millie's willpower to push away from him.

She gripped the bridge of her nose, closed her eyes and tried to get her breathing back under control.

'Morning, Mils.'

His just-woke-up voice was deeper and rougher, sexier. And, no, he shouldn't shorten her name, making it sound sexy and sweet. *Be strong, Millie. He's your boss.*

'*Mr* De Rossi.'

Taz squinted at her and pushed his hand through his messy hair. His jaw was rough with stubble, and the pillow crease on his left cheek made him seem a little less of a bossy billionaire. More approachable and, damn it, lovable.

Get it together, Millie! 'I was just checking your schedule. You've got quite a bit to do before we leave for the polo tournament,' she stated, her tone a little sharp.

His dark-lashed eyelids dropped, and his lips tightened. Right, he wasn't happy with her cool greeting. Well, tough. They'd been out of line last night, and they needed normal this morning. 'No *Good morning, darling, how did you sleep?*'

Oh, the man had a PhD in sarcasm. 'Good morning, Mr De Rossi,' she politely parroted, tipping her head to the side. 'How did you sleep?'

He scowled at her, slapped his hands on his hips and straightened his back. Ah, the warrior pose, designed to intimidate. 'What happened from the time you left until this morning?' he demanded, his normal brusqueness back in his voice. 'Did you not get any sleep?'

She might as well bite the bullet and get them back on a professional footing. 'What happened was that I came to my senses and remembered that we work together and that I am not prepared to be another of your conquests.'

Taz cocked his head to one side, and his gaze bore into her. 'I need a gallon of coffee before we have this conversation,' he stated, gesturing to the coffee machine sitting on the kitchen's Italian marble counter. 'Make me one, will you?'

When she hesitated, he raised a thick black brow. 'You work for me, right? Espresso, double, black.'

He'd manoeuvred her into a corner, leaving her with no option but to play by his rules. It was annoying how easily Taz could trip her up. His fantastic looks, sheer masculinity and raw sexuality meant that she often overlooked how sharp he was and how effortlessly he wielded words like weapons. He was quick, cunning and unaccustomed to anyone refusing to dance to the beat of his drum.

Millie thought fast. She could argue against making him coffee, implying that she thought herself more than his employee, or she could make the coffee, reinforcing the idea that she was nothing more than hired help. Devil, meet deep blue sea.

Damn him for making her question everything. For making her doubt herself.

It was important to stand her ground and reinforce their boundaries. She needed to be smart, to think with her head. She couldn't let her libido hijack her common sense. Last night had been a mistake, a universe-rearranging mistake, and it wasn't one she intended to repeat.

So with gritted teeth, Millie made his double espresso and placed the cup on the coffee table next to him. He didn't say thank you but just smirked at her. He was testing her. *Great.*

Walking into his bedroom, she ignored his huge, messy bed, just managing to stop herself from imagining how amazing it would be to share that with him, and walked into his enormous closet. The hotel staff had unpacked his luggage, and they'd arranged his shirts per colour, his pants and suits too. He had at least fifteen pairs of shoes on the shoe rack. He was in town for ten days: How many pairs of shoes did one man need? Unable to help herself, she picked up his cologne, took a deep breath and sighed.

She was getting distracted and more than a little turned-on. Irritated, she pulled the first T-shirt from a perfectly aligned pile and carried it back through to the lounge, draping it over his shoulder. 'Please get dressed.'

He ignored her and scrolled through his phone. One of these days, she'd brain him with it. Reaching for her iPad on the table, she flipped it open and waited for Taz to pull on his shirt. It lay on his tanned, muscular shoulder, and she knew he was waiting for her to push him to get dressed. She wasn't going to give him the satisfaction.

Summoning her most professional voice, she ran through his schedule for the morning and ignored his surly responses. He didn't like hearing the word *no*. He'd simply have to get used to it. Their sleeping together was not going to happen.

Sex with Taz would blur the lines, make things far too complicated. She was already acting as his girlfriend; she didn't need thorough research to nail the part. As far as she could tell, if she giggled, made the occasional innocuous comment and looked adoringly at Taz, she'd fulfil her end of the bargain.

'Are you going to answer me or not?'

Millie lifted her head, doing a mental rewind. Right, he'd asked her something about what she was wearing to the polo tournament. 'Your stylist sent over a couple of dresses. I'm leaning toward a brown-and-white maxi halter-neck dress...'

He looked thoroughly disinterested. Why ask a question if he wasn't going to listen to the answer?

Millie sighed. Was this her fault? She'd asked him to treat her as one of his staff, and that was what he was doing. She couldn't complain about it now. 'I won't embarrass you, if that's what you're wondering.'

His eyes lifted and slammed into hers. 'I wasn't.'

He was properly pissed. Millie closed her laptop and placed it on the coffee table. They had to spend time together, today and over the next few weeks, and they couldn't snap and snarl at each other. They needed to clear the air. 'Look, Taz, we can't sleep together and work together. I can't be your assistant one minute and your girlfriend the next. It's too confusing.'

And I can't afford to lose track of who I am at any time and let the two bleed into each other. On one hand, she might end up doing a terrible job as his PR person and miss something crucial or, even worse, she might find attraction turning into, God forbid, *like*. Maybe even more. Was she overthinking this? Taz had made it very clear earlier that he wasn't interested in anything more than sex, and she'd grown up witnessing two highly dysfunctional marriages, so long-term wasn't for her. But something held her back. 'This situation is complicated enough without us adding the gasoline of sex to the bonfire.'

His expression remained impassive. 'Fine.'

She threw up her hands, frustrated. 'Is that all you are going to say?'

Turbulent eyes met hers. 'You want to keep things

professional, I'm saying okay. What more do you need from me?'

He drained his coffee, pushed the cup in her direction and stood. 'Get rid of that and order a high protein breakfast from room service. I want it delivered in an hour. I'm going to head down to the hotel gym to work out.'

'You have a broken wrist—'

'Not your problem.'

Taz walked away from her, and Millie twisted her lips. Right. Message received. She'd tapped the brakes, and he'd brought the race to a complete stop. She should be pleased. That was what she wanted.

Then, why did she feel so exasperated? And, worse, frustrated?

CHAPTER EIGHT

THE POLO MATCH WAS, essentially, a picnic on steroids—where lemonade was swapped for Moët et Chandon Champagne, PB & J sandwiches for blinis, and jam doughnuts for exquisite patisseries. Designer labels replaced ripped board shorts and battered T-shirts, and inane chatter masqueraded as conversation. Insincere compliments were casually lobbed conversational grenades.

Taz, naturally, was a hit, parrying compliments and questions with effortless charm, utterly polished and charismatic, eliciting sighs and swoons from his captive audience.

Wearing stone-coloured chinos and a navy linen jacket over a crisp white shirt he looked ridiculously good. He hadn't bothered shaving, and the thick stubble suited him far too well. A green-and-blue pocket square peeked out from his jacket, and every so often, the silver bracelets on either side of his Patek Philippe watch caught the sunlight. His taste—or his stylist's taste—was, Millie begrudgingly admitted, impeccable.

She took a sip of champagne and remembered attending a polo match when she was a child. Her mother had insisted on her wearing a white dress and white shoes and got annoyed when both got splattered with mud. She'd been ordered to spend the rest of the afternoon in the car, which suited her fine as she'd stashed her book under the passenger seat. Just another instance of her not being about to live up to their impossibly high expectations. She was constantly set up to fail.

Millie had expected to feel like a fish out of water at this event, but she managed to exchange small talk, side-step questions about Taz and even engage in a conversation about polo. She wasn't half as bored or on edge as she'd thought she'd be. Taz was the centre of attention, and that meant eyes on her too, but she was handling standing in the spotlight better than she'd expected. It wasn't the nightmare she expected it to be. Maybe some of those old insecurities had faded, or maybe she'd simply grown up. Either way, not feeling like she was dancing on the edge of a sharp blade was a pleasant surprise.

Millie jerked when Taz's arm snaked around her waist, pulling her flush against him. She barely had time to blink before he dipped his head, his lips brushing her temple. The warm weight of his kiss lingered as he spoke softly, his words pitched low for her ears alone.

'I'm bored, and this is tedious,' he murmured, sounding irritated. 'How much longer?'

'You *have* to watch the first game and should watch the second,' Millie told him, inhaling his scent.

'Watching and not playing is torture,' he muttered, his grip on her hip tightening.

Taz was a man of action, and she understood his frustration. He wasn't the type to stand on the sidelines. She patted his bicep. 'Hang in there,' she told him. 'Being here benefits you and the charity. It's a win-win scenario. Keep your eye on the prize.'

He pulled back and looked down at her, and her heart stuttered at his expression. 'I'd rather keep my eyes on you.'

An image of her naked on his lap last night flashed behind her eyes, and her cheeks heated. 'Taz...people are looking at us,' she murmured, heat in her cheeks.

The corner of his mouth lifted into a sexy smirk. 'I know,' he told her, cupping her face in his hands. His eyes glinted with a curious combination of lust and amusement. 'We want them to look at us, remember?'

Her protest was captured then smothered by his lips. His tongue slipped between her teeth, and the world faded away. He took control of their kiss, and there was nothing she could do but respond. Nothing she *wanted* to do but respond.

Taz abruptly ended the kiss and looked down at her with hooded eyes and a satisfied smile. 'Give it a minute and we'll be all over social media,' he stated. 'The bad boy and the good girl.'

Millie resisted the urge to touch her lips with her fingertips and worked hard to keep her scowl off her face. He'd kissed her to make a point. Millie sighed. He was punishing her for pulling away this morning, for putting them in opposite corners of the ring. He'd been happy to wait for the right moment to retaliate, patient enough to make sure she was on the back foot, sneaky enough to make her feel unstable.

He was unlike anyone she'd met before. Oh, her parents were self-assured, not shy about putting themselves forward, but Taz was so confident, possessing an arrogance and self-belief she'd never encountered before. He knew exactly who he was and what he was doing. If her family was a garden bonfire, then Taz was an out-of-control wildfire. He didn't singe and scorch; he annihilated everything in his path.

Millie felt like she was facing that raging fire holding a watering can.

Taz's low curse had Millie instantly on high alert. She turned to see who'd captured his attention and saw a polo player, dressed in white jodhpurs and a branded shirt, slapping his knee-high riding boot with his leather crop. Hanging onto his hand, like she was the survivor of a shipwreck and he the life ring, was a pale lanky exceptionally pretty redhead.

And Millie knew, with the feminine wisdom she didn't know she possessed up until now, that this woman and Taz had seen each other naked.

Jealously, hot and acid, burned her stomach lining, and she was annoyed at her gut response. She was his employee and fake girlfriend, and while they'd allowed things to get a little out of control last night, she had no right to feel jealous.

Taz murmured a low *Here comes trouble*, and on seeing the polo player's face—hard, defiant and thoroughly annoyed—Millie knew he was right.

'You slept with her, right?' she muttered out of the side of his mouth.

'Yes,' he admitted, unembarrassed. 'She told me they were done. It turned out things weren't as cut and dry as she said they were.'

'Is he going to make trouble?' she whispered.

'Highly possible.'

Damn it, the day had been going well so far. Lots of the attendees had pledged to make donations to the nominated charity—a fund for the victims of natural disasters such as flooding and hurricanes. A fight between the guest of honour and what looked to be the captain of one of the polo teams would be disastrous, especially since Taz was finally, *finally*, generating some decent press.

'De Rossi.'

'Bertolo.'

The two men gripped hands, their fingers turning white with pressure. She caught the redhead's eye and saw her quick wince. Right, she wasn't imagining their death-by-handshake duel.

Millie shoulder-bumped Taz in what she hoped was a playful way and held out her hand for the polo player to shake. He had no choice but to release Taz's hand: a good thing, because she knew how stubborn Taz could be. Without her intervention, they'd stand there for hours. 'I'm Millie, Taz's girlfriend.'

'Brody Bertolo.' He gave her hand a quick shake and placed his hands on his hips. He nodded at Taz's arm. 'It's a pity you're injured, or else I would've suggested you play a chukka with us. If you lasted the seven minutes, I would've made a substantial donation to your charity.'

What a jerk! Millie sent him the sweetest smile she could muster. 'Why don't you make the donation and we skip Taz getting on a horse?' she asked, trying to hide her dislike.

'I could still play, even with a broken hand,' Taz smoothly replied. 'How much are we talking?'

God save her from idiotic men. He had limited use of his fingers, with only his thumb working on his broken hand. How would he control a horse and hold a mallet? It was a stupid comment, and stupidity wasn't something she associated with Taz. Their interaction had drawn a curious crowd, suggesting that Taz and the redhead's affair had been a topic of hot conversation amongst the polo-playing set. And Red was looking a little smug at all the attention.

'A cool half a mil?' Brody asked.

'You'll give the charity five hundred thousand if I last a chukka?' Taz clarified.

'But you have to take part. You can't stay on the side-lines,' Brody countered.

It was a huge donation, and as Taz tipped his head to the side, Millie knew he was considering his suggestion.

He gestured to his clothes. 'I'd need proper clothes.'

Millie's mouth dropped open. Had he lost his mind? Getting on a horse with a broken hand, to take part in one of the most competitive sports in the world, was an absurd idea.

'And if you don't last the chukka, you donate a half million to the charity,' Brody suggested, a half sneer, half smile on his face.

'Deal.'

Millie couldn't keep quiet a minute longer. 'You do know he's an F1 racer, not a polo player, right?'

Everyone laughed, and Millie knew she was the butt of the joke. She swallowed the urge to remind them she was head of Taz's PR and that she knew his sporting history. But she was here as his adoring girlfriend, not his PR representative.

The redhead sent her a pitying smile. 'You're obviously new on the scene, and not part of the polo set.' Millie's nails dug into her skin at her condescending tone. She sounded like her mum and aunt.

'Everyone knows that Taz was one of the most promising polo players in the world when he was in his teens,' Red said, her nose in the air.

Yes, she *knew* that. Millie forced herself to place her open hand above her heart and widen her eyes. 'Oh, I thought he was a scratch golf player and was considering going pro.' She looked at Taz. 'Did I get that wrong, *darling*?'

He shrugged. 'I had options.'

Many options, it seemed. But he chose racing. It was, after all, the family business.

'Are you doing this or not, De Rossi?'

Oh, hell no, he wasn't. Before Taz could agree to this asinine scheme, she'd clocked the *Challenge accepted* in his eyes, slipped her hand into his and smiled. 'I'm sorry, but would you excuse us for a minute?'

'Hold on, Millie,' Taz growled.

She dug her fingernails into the top of his hand. 'I'm sure Mr Bertolo could give us five minutes.'

Irritation rolled off him, but he pulled her out of earshot and put his back to the group congregating around Bertolo and the redhead. His big frame shielded her, so she glared up at him. 'What do you think you are doing?' she hissed. 'You cannot get up on a horse! He's taunting you, Taz.'

'So?'

'So you can walk away.'

'And look like he's got the better of me? That's not happening.'

'What if you fall off?'

'I've been riding since I was three. I don't fall off horses.'

She only had one argument left. 'The press will get wind of this. Everyone's phone cameras are already out, waiting to film you. It will be uploaded online within five minutes of you settling into the saddle, probably less. Whether you win the bet or not, the press will slant their reports to say that you are reckless, that you are risking your recovery to one-up a polo player. They will say your ego can't handle losing, that you aren't taking your recovery seriously, and that if you really wanted to win the championship, you'd never risk it on such a stupid bet! You're a target, so don't give them bullets to shoot at you.'

She could tell he wanted to argue, and Millie waited for his scalpel-sharp response. How would she spin this when it hit the press in the morning, what excuse could she conjure? Whatever she came up with would be weak, because the most logical explanation was that he was an egotistical idiot.

What was it with this man's need to be the best at everything all the time? Why couldn't he back down, step away? Why was he constantly waging battles or engaging in skirmishes? It was almost as if he went out of his way to prove that he was better, stronger, the best of the best. How many people were scratch golfers, ace polo players and Formula One drivers? To be good at one was amazing, to be good at so many things took dedication and hard work and perseverance. Why would he put himself through that? What drove him to excel?

Behind the irritation and the determination was more than a hint of misery. And desperation.

He met her eyes and rubbed his hand over his chin. 'I can't back down, Millie.'

A part of her wanted to roll her eyes and say *Of course you can!* but she knew he didn't want to feel like Bertolo had an edge over him. Why? She didn't know. He was a billionaire owner of a racing team, and Bertolo was a professional polo player. On the wealth and social hierarchy, Bertolo was a bug beneath his shoe.

But if she didn't come up with a solution, she knew Taz would take the bet. So she needed to find one, and pronto. Guess she wasn't only going to earn her million pounds by playing his adoring girlfriend.

She thought fast. 'Be honest. Tell him you can't risk any further injury to your hand, but when the cast comes off, after you win your fourth championship, you are fully prepared to take on his challenge. As a measure of your commitment, you'll donate a half million to the charity now, and you'll bet another half million. I could organise a charity polo day, he can choose a team, you can choose a team, and we'll choose a charity, and your fans can bet on the outcome. You'll both get credit and some good PR.'

He pondered her response before handing her a look saturated with approval. It felt like the warm, early morning sun on her face. How amazing would it be if he could look at her like that for the rest of her life? *Oh, Millie, you're in such deep trouble.*

'I can live with that.' Taz nodded.

Millie released the breath she'd been holding. 'What else can I expect from you? A fencer to challenge you to a sword fight, a swimmer suggesting you swim the English Channel? Is there anything you can't do?' she asked, as he stroked her cheek.

'Apparently, I can't get you back into my bed again.'

She remembered the hint of vulnerability in his eyes, the chink in his armour of arrogance. That smidgen of insecurity made him all the more attractive. It also made her feel more self-confident and braver. He'd told her, clearly, that whatever they did in bed had no connection to her work as his PR officer or as her acting as his girlfriend. She believed him. She couldn't use either as an excuse.

Truth was, she didn't want an excuse. Did she even *need* one? She was a consenting adult who was allowed to have some bedroom-based fun. The fizzy feelings Taz raised in her made her feel powerfully feminine and femininely powerful. When he looked at her like *that*, all thoughts of being less-than and feeling insecure disappeared, and her self-doubt faded away. He made her braver…

And wasn't being brave what she was trying to achieve?

'I think that could be arranged,' she whispered.

Taz smiled, and Millie knew she'd hopped from the frying pan into earth's molten core. Sure, sleeping with him might be a mistake, but if it was, she'd own it. Because, for the first time, she was choosing to be with a man because of her burning attraction, and not because she felt lonely or needed reassurance.

And for her, right now, that was huge.

Hours later and back in his luxurious South Beach hotel suite, Taz was still curious as to why Millie had changed her mind. He'd tossed out the suggestion of taking her to bed more in hope than in expectation, and her agreement had surprised the hell out of him. And he was a man not easily surprised. His gaze drifted over her lush body, and he hardened instantly. He'd ask her later; right now he wanted to give his full attention to this sexy, stunning woman in his bed.

Millie's skin was so soft, endlessly creamy and lightly fragranced. She was, possibly, the most feminine woman he'd ever met. Taz stroked the back of his knuckles from her neck to her stomach, and her eyes fluttered closed as her back arched to his touch.

She was so responsive, so into him and what he did, in a way few of his lovers had been before. Many had been track bunnies, more interested in bragging rights than sexual pleasure, and others hoped sex was a gateway to accessing his lifestyle. But Millie was fully and utterly present in the moment, lost in how he made her feel.

Her response brought an intensity to sex that had been missing for a long, long time. For far too long it had been a way to blow off steam, a form of escape. Sex with Millie was…more. Taz lowered his mouth to swirl his tongue around her nipple, smiling when her fingers tunnelled into his hair to hold his head to her breast. Surprisingly, Millie wasn't afraid to show him who she was, what she liked and how she felt. He adored her honesty.

More than that, he liked that she was smart and sensible and, albeit temporarily, solidly in his corner. She'd been right earlier: Playing polo would've been a stupid move. Oh, he knew he could've won the bet—that would've been the easy part—but the public reaction would've been swift and brutal. No, as hard as it was to admit, Millie had made the right call and presented him with a solution that enabled him to walk away with his pride intact.

His father's constant comparisons to Alex made him want to be the best at everything, all the time. In his head, he wasn't only competing against Alex but against everyone else. That's what happened when your father considered you as a spare part, as second best, as unimportant. As a teenager, he'd needed to be the best at everything in the vague hope that his father might notice and be impressed. He was better than Alex at every sport, but that didn't matter to his dad. He wasn't Alex.

And why was he thinking about his father when he had this sensational woman in his bed? She'd agreed to sleep with him and wanted to be with him, and he owed her the courtesy of his full attention. But if he allowed himself to deeply dive into her, if he didn't keep some emotional guard-rails up, he might go too deep and not resurface. And if he did, he might come back less…

Detached? Unemotional? More connected?

Taz shook his head, frustrated at the thoughts leaking through his normally impenetrable shields. *Cut it out, De Rossi.* He looked at the tiny triangle of lace that could barely be considered underwear and ran his finger over the fabric, sliding between her legs. Her panties were already soaked, so he sat on his knees and pulled them down her hips, smiling when she lifted her butt cheek to allow him to push them down her legs. He tossed them over his shoulder, thinking that he needed to strip. Sex was more fun when both parties were naked.

But he could look at her for hours: She was pleasure personified. From her messy hair to her freckled chest and lust-soaked eyes, her flushed cheeks and rounded stomach and hips, she was all woman.

And for the moment, all his.

Millie picked up his hand and placed it between her thighs, and he was surprised and turned-on by her boldness. Her silent demand was unexpected. And hot. Was some of his sexual confidence rubbing off on her? He slid his finger over and around her, smiling when she pulled her bottom lip between her teeth. Her fingers went to her breast, and she tugged her nipple, trying to maximise her pleasure. She was being selfish, wanting this moment to be about her and only her...

Good for her. He liked people who knew what they wanted and went for it.

'That's it, Millie. Keep touching yourself,' he encouraged her, moving off the bed. Without undressing, he placed his hands under her thighs and pulled her to the edge of the bed, pushing her knees apart and revealing her, pink and swollen, to his gaze. So, so pretty.

He dropped to his knees and lowered his mouth to her. She arched off the bed, and he placed his hand on her stomach to pin her in place while he worked one finger, then another, into her heat.

He was rock hard, harder than he could ever remember being as he softly sucked her. As his fingers plunged in and out of her, he thought about how he wanted to take her after she came hard on his tongue and fingers. From behind? Her on top? There were so many options but...

What he most wanted was to keep it simple. He wanted to watch her eyes as he entered her, as he brought her to another orgasm, their eyes staying connected. He wanted to see her fall apart, and he'd come as she did. For one blissful moment, one person, the same pleasure. He couldn't remember when last that had happened...or whether it ever had.

Impatient, he pulled back and quickly stripped. Millie thrashed her head on the pillow, and when her hand headed to her core, he pulled it back and firmly commanded her to wait for him. They'd do this together.

After sliding on a condom with more haste than grace, he lowered himself to her. Her legs fell apart, and she moaned when the tip of his cock found her entrance. It took all his willpower not to surge inside her, to bury himself to the hilt.

'Millie, look at me.'

Panting, she tried to arch her hips to pull him in, but he was in charge. They were doing this on his timescale, not hers. He pulled back and her eyes flew open, frustrated. 'Keep your eyes on mine. You close them or you look away, I'll stop.'

As if in challenge, Millie tried to touch herself again. Knowing how close she was, he pulled her hand and clamped it to her side. If he had the use of his other hand, he'd hold her wrists above her head, but his threat of stopping would have to be enough.

'Don't touch yourself, don't look away, and you'll only come when I tell you that you can.'

'*Tazio.*'

Oh, man, the way she said his full name, it was a shot of adrenaline straight into his spine. Unable to wait, he plunged deep inside her, and her heat engulfed him from tip to root. He wanted to make love to her without the barrier of a condom, but despite the thin layer of latex between him, he was consumed by her heat. He knew she was close, and that it wouldn't take much to make her come, but he wanted to draw out this experience, to make it memorable, to stand out from the many sexual encounters he'd had before.

Because this wasn't a mating ritual, this was… God, he didn't know what it was. But he did know he wanted to remember the changing colours in her eyes, the slick of moisture on her lips, the flush in her cheeks and the staggering heat rolling off them.

The room smelled of sex and her perfume, of the calla lilies in the huge vase on the dresser, of clean sheets and sexy woman. A gentle, always-warm Miami sea-breeze blew over their bodies.

'Taz, please, you've got to start moving,' Millie said, tiny pants accompanying her words. 'I *need* you.'

He knew she meant that she needed him right at this moment, needed him to make her feel good and to give her the orgasm he'd promised. But he was, shockingly, entertaining the thought that he needed more from her than just sex.

Why was he going there? Why was he making this more than it was? This could only be the start of a fling, at best, a short-lived affair. They had tonight, but tomorrow they'd say goodbye and would only meet up in Italy for the Grand Prix in Imola in ten days.

He was overthinking…well, everything.

No, this was about sex, pure and simple. So he pumped his hips, stroking her with all the pent-up fury and confusion that had been building since he'd first set eyes on her. He slipped his good hand under her butt, lifted her hips and went a little deeper, a little harder.

But even as her body dissolved around him, as she panted, moaned and screamed through her release, even as he erupted into her, her eyes didn't leave his.

And neither did his.

* * *

Taz handed Millie a bottle of water from the hotel's bar fridge before climbing back into bed beside her. He took a long sip from his own, utterly at ease, while her mind remained chaotic and her body hummed.

Bells still rang in her ears, and her skin thrummed with aftershocks from the most intense orgasm of her life. She felt turned inside out, upside down and completely undone. What on earth had happened? That wasn't just good sex. It was earth-shatteringly, soul-stealingly unforgettable.

Taz's hand found her wrist, his touch grounding her. She looked down as he fiddled with the tiny silver racing car dangling from her heavy link, silver bracelet. The charm was subtle, almost unnoticeable, but Taz's sharp eyes had zeroed in on it.

'When did you get this?' he asked, lifting her arm to inspect the charm more closely.

She smiled softly, the memory bittersweet. 'It was Ben's. He used to tie it to the laces of his shoes before every race.'

His hand dropped, resting on her thigh as he leaned back against the headboard, his hand behind his head. The pose was casual, masculine and infuriatingly sexy. 'I remember now,' he said thoughtfully. 'I also remember him losing it once before Silverstone. He was normally so laid-back that the news of him being in a state because he'd lost his lucky charm reached the other drivers. He was, apparently, unbearable until he found it again.'

She chuckled. 'When I was four, I gave him a plastic one from a Christmas cracker. He had a jeweller recreate it in silver.' She ran her fingers over the tiny car, the charm swinging slightly from its link. 'Ben's parents claimed his body after his death, and this charm was on him when he died. I asked his parents for it, and luckily they gave it to me before his will was read or I would never have got it.'

Taz frowned. 'What do you mean?'

'I was Ben's sole heir, and his parents were enraged they weren't mentioned in his will. Then they heard I was planning to donate all his cash to a charity set up in his name, and they went ballistic. They challenged the will and took me to court.'

Taz raised an eyebrow, his olive-brown skin glowing against the pure white sheets. 'I presume you won?'

'It was a long, hard slog, but I did. Eventually." Millie tapped the charm, smiling softly. 'Luckily, I had emails from Ben, where he talked about the up-and-coming drivers he was helping, how he wanted to do more, so I could prove I was acting in accordance with his wishes.'

'How's your relationship with Ben's parents now?' Taz asked.

Millie sighed. 'I haven't spoken to them since the judge ruled in my favour. And because my parents supported my aunt and uncle's bid to contest the will, my relationship with my parents is frosty.'

Taz squeezed her knee, a silent gesture of comfort.

'I liked Ben,' Taz quietly stated. 'And I think he was good for Alex.'

Millie tilted her head, immediately curious. 'What do you mean?'

Taz hesitated, his gaze drifting to the lilies on the dresser. Their sweet scent filled the room, a sharp contrast to the tension that had sprung up between them. 'Ben was grounded. Sensible. Alex needed that.'

It wasn't what she'd expected to hear. 'Alex seemed to

be pretty grounded and sensible already,' she said, pressing for more.

Taz shrugged dismissively, his expression turning remote. 'I don't talk about Alex.'

The statement was blunt and final, but she couldn't leave it alone. If he hadn't wanted to talk about his brother, why bring him into the conversation? 'You should. He's your brother.' Her voice softened. 'Losing him like that must've been terrible.'

Taz's jaw tightened, but his silence was as loud as a foghorn. He'd pulled back, and she couldn't help feeling hurt at his sudden emotional distance. She knew she shouldn't: There was nothing between them but chemistry, a fake relationship and a business deal. Despite knowing that, understanding that, she still desperately wanted him to trust her enough to open up to her. She reached out, brushing her fingers over the back of his hand. 'I'm so sorry, Taz.'

He didn't respond, but his hand tightened briefly over hers before he sat up and drained his water bottle, tossing it neatly into the waste-basket.

'Show-off,' she muttered, trying to lighten the mood.

He smirked, the tension easing slightly. 'I'm multitalented.'

She could attest to that. Millie let her fingers trail over his hand, marvelling at the contrast between its strength and gentleness. These hands had given her so much pleasure—but they were also hands that could steer a car at rocket-like speed over twisty tracks.

'How do you feel about going to Imola?' he asked abruptly. 'Are you going to be okay?'

Her chest tightened at the mention of the track where

Ben had died. 'I don't know,' she admitted. 'I thought I'd be fine, but every time I think about it…' She swallowed hard. 'But I have to be there. It's my job. I feel so guilty I didn't see him before he died, but I'm so glad I didn't witness his crash, Taz,' she added.

'Me too, Mils.' Taz ran a hand over her shoulder, soothing and steady. He pulled her close, her cheek resting against his chest. His warmth, his presence, was an unexpected balm to her frayed nerves.

'Families are so complicated,' she murmured, her hand resting on his ridged stomach.

'Aren't they?' he agreed, his hand covering hers.

But his touch, his proximity, stirred something more profound. Slowly, her hand drifted lower, her fingers trailing over the hard ridges of his stomach to his erection. Her fist encircled him, he hardened, and Millie felt, for the first time, powerful at raising such a quick response in such an alpha man. It was such a confidence-booster, but despite her increasing self-assurance, she knew she still had a way to go before she felt wholly at ease in her skin, secure in this world she now moved in.

And that was work she had to do. No man, not Ben and not Tazio De Rossi, could do that for her.

Two things could happen at once… While she worked on herself and learned to stand up straight and be strong, she could enjoy him and enjoy their off-the-charts attraction.

'Whether they're complicated or not,' she said, her voice low, 'this…*isn't*.'

She did not doubt that tomorrow would bring its own problems, but tonight, being with him was all that mattered.

CHAPTER NINE

Imola, Italy

TWELVE DAYS LATER, at the Autodromo Internazionale Enzo e Dino Ferrari, Taz inspected the track with his drivers, debriefed the race engineers and strategists, and held a video conference with his research team in the UK. By mid-afternoon, he'd put in more than a full day's work. Yet his temper simmered as he fielded endless questions from his employees, colleagues and the press about Millie's whereabouts.

Before he'd had a chance to suggest that they meet up in London during the break, Millie told him she'd see him in Italy, and he hadn't seen her since. As she'd done during the Shanghai race, Millie slid into his thoughts far too often and usually at inopportune moments. His thoughts often went to what Millie was doing, thinking, *eating* for God's sake! For the first time in his life, being apart from his lover annoyed him. That he missed her irritated him even more. Exchanging work emails and brief PR-related calls didn't cut it.

For the first time he could remember, the *only* time, work had competition for his attention.

Taz rubbed the back of his neck. Millie'd arrived in

Italy six hours ago; she should've been at the track for hours now, but he'd yet to lay eyes on her. Where was she? They might be lovers, but he knew Millie well enough to know that her pride wouldn't let her slack off on the job. And her job meant being at his side or, at the very least, within earshot.

Had some PR disaster occurred he wasn't yet aware of? Was she putting out PR fires? Or was she ill? She'd been working long, long hours in a high stress environment. He was a demanding boss and expected results. Was she finding the work—him—overwhelming?

Taz checked his watch, shook his head and clenched his jaw. He wouldn't find the answers to his questions here. He had a few free hours before the sponsor dinner, enough time to track Millie down and ask her directly. He barked a command at an intern, instructing him to organise a courtesy car to be waiting for him at the turnstiles.

Sliding his aviator shades onto his face, he raked a hand through his hair and strode through the exit. The roar of the gathered fans was deafening, the flashes from cameras cutting through the overcast sky. Hopefully his sunglasses masked his anxiety. He wasn't used to worrying about anyone, ever, and he was exasperated Millie could make him feel this way.

But the world didn't need to know any of that.

As he stepped into the parking lot, his eyebrows rose. Parked a yard away was a sleek, limited-edition Ferrari, a beast of a machine. This was his courtesy car? Nice. Not enough to lift his mood, but nice.

He took the fob the olive-skinned brunette held out to him and ignored her sexy smile.

He slid behind the wheel and ran his hands over the

leather steering wheel. The interior was immaculate, the idling engine a low-throated growl as he tapped the start button. He punched the accelerator, the roar of the car rolling over the crowd. His fans bellowed their approval.

Precision and power. He might have to buy one of these for himself.

Ten minutes later, Taz pulled up in front of the boutique hotel where he and Millie were staying while in Italy. Killing the engine, he stepped out and pushed his sunglasses into his hair.

Striding up the stone steps to the small but luxurious lobby, he spotted the hotel manager. With a flick of his wrist, he slapped the key fob into the man's hand.

'Move this for me, will you?'

The man looked from Taz to the Ferrari parked under his portico, his eyes sparkling with appreciation. 'Sì, signore. It will be my pleasure.'

'I understand that Ms James has checked in. Where is she?' he demanded, hooking the arm of his sunglasses into the V of his shirt.

'I believe she is on the back patio.'

Taz nodded. If someone had told him, a few weeks back, that he, the team owner and its principal driver, the most essential component of De Rossi, would be chasing down one of his employees, he would've rolled his eyes. He'd would've snapped terse explanation: he was paying her salary and would demand to know why she wasn't at the racetrack, doing her job.

Work always came first. Vesuvius could erupt, an asteroid could strike, but his team and the De Rossi brand were everyone's number one priority.

But he knew Millie well enough, and trusted her just

enough, to know she'd have a damn good reason for not being at the track. Something was wrong. He knew it like he knew his own signature.

Taz stepped onto the back patio, his eyes immediately sweeping over the space. Thick, ancient vines tossed shade over the area, shielding it from the summer sun. It was a peaceful retreat, a world away from the chaos of the racetrack. In the far corner sat a low-slung comfortable two-seater couch, paired with a sleek coffee table. Millie was curled up in the corner, her legs tucked beneath her, a laptop open on her knees.

She was absorbed, her brows drawn together in concentration, fingers poised above the keyboard. She was dressed in a pair of form-fitting hot pink tailored shorts and an oversize button-down shirt, sleeves rolled up. Her hair caught the soft light filtering through the vines, and he experienced a punch of lust and a now-familiar hit of need.

He leaned against the door-frame for a moment, watching her, feeling the heat of his anxiety wrestle with something else entirely—a pull he didn't want to acknowledge. He ignored the profound whisper of *There she is*. No, this wasn't the time for fanciful bullshit. He needed a reset, immediately. This was about work, and her being AWOL today. When she finally noticed him, Millie would have to justify why she'd skipped work and disappeared when she was most needed.

'Where have you been? And why aren't you answering your phone?'

Millie's head shot up, and her eyes widened. 'Taz…'

He walked over to her, telling himself he had to treat her like he would any other employee. 'Your PR position requires you to be trackside, with *me*. I don't recall a clause stating that you can hang out at the hotel!'

Millie looked away and lifted her hand to her forehead, covering her eyes. He frowned. There was no avoiding it: he was definitely missing something. He couldn't remember Millie ever taking a day off and slacking on the job before. She routinely worked long hours and didn't complain. 'Are you sick? Do you have a migraine?'

She shook her head but kept her eyes on her screen, her bottom lip between her teeth. Concern replaced the last vestiges of irritation. 'Millie, look at me,' he softly commanded.

It took her a while to obey his order, and she couldn't meet his eyes, looking at the base of his throat instead. He skimmed his eyes over her face, taking in her red, swollen eyes and her pink nose. She was either having an allergic reaction or…

'Have you been crying?' he asked.

Her small shrug answered that question. Taz silently cursed and rocked on his feet. He didn't engage with people emotionally and rarely had personal conversations. He didn't have the faintest idea how to ask her why she'd cried hard enough to leave traces of tears on her face. Her bottom lip was still wobbling, for God's sake!

'What's wrong? Why the tears?' he demanded, wincing at his too-harsh tone. He prayed she didn't start crying again. He wasn't a fan of emotions and didn't know how to handle a crying woman. Normally he walked away and either left them to get on with it or…

Truthfully, there wasn't an *or*. He never bothered to engage.

Taz looked at the door leading into the hotel and calculated he could be inside in three seconds and back at the car in five, at Imola in fifteen minutes. He knew what he was doing there.

Here?

Not a bit.

But this was Millie, and because she was hurting, the heart he didn't know he possessed ached a little too. Walking away was not an option so he'd have to man up. If he could dice death on a racetrack at three hundred miles per hour, he could do this too.

Maybe.

He rubbed the back of his neck and walked to stand between the coffee table and the couch. Closing her laptop, he pushed it to the side and shoved the table back, making room for his long legs. Sitting on the table he faced her, and up close he could see her road-map red eyes.

'Talk to me, Millie.'

Millie unfolded her legs and rested her forearms on her knees. 'We both know that you'd much rather be anywhere else but here, Taz,' she said with all the charm of a snapping turtle.

She was looking to pick a fight, and he didn't blame her. It was so much easier to be angry than vulnerable. 'Why the tears, Millie?' he quietly asked. 'And I'm not moving until I get an answer.'

'Ben...'

Ben? What about him? Her shoulders slumped, and her head dropped, and she played with the silver charm on her bracelet. The charm that Ben always tied to the shoelaces of his racing boot. The charm Ben had been wearing when he crashed at...

Taz swallowed his harsh curse. Ben had died at Imola.

His car had spun out and he was dead before the medics could get to him.

But because he was selfish and self-absorbed, and incredibly busy and highly stressed, he'd forgotten. God, of course Millie would find it difficult to go back to the place where Ben died, to be able to pinpoint the spot where his life ended. Taz rubbed his hands over his face, embarrassed at his lack of awareness. Confused by his need to comfort and protect.

And maybe it was time for him to admit that the real reason he'd left the track, and his responsibilities, was because he needed to be with Millie and was desperate to connect with her. That he'd missed her, and not only in his bed. He'd missed her steadying influence, her wry humour and the way she kept his feet firmly on the ground.

But this wasn't about him and what he needed from her. Faced with visiting the site where Ben had lost his life, the person she'd loved the most, Millie was in a world of hurt. And that was an acid-tipped knife in his soul.

She used the ball of her hand to blot away her tears. 'I thought I'd be fine, but I couldn't make myself go to the track today. I mean, I know I need to, it's my *job*. I also want to lay flowers where he died. But I couldn't muster the courage today.'

He could throw himself into the tightest of corners at three hundred miles an hour and make split-second decisions that risked a car worth several fortunes and the livelihoods of two thousand employees across his racing and technology divisions. But when faced with Millie's tear-streaked cheeks and eyes saturated with pain, Taz felt utterly out of his depth.

She lifted those shattered eyes to his. 'I feel like such

a coward, Taz.' Her voice cracked, and he winced. Her raw honesty drilled into him, through him.

His hands itched to comfort her, to stroke her hair, to tuck the damp strands clinging to her face behind her ears. But he held back. There were different kinds of bravery, and Taz knew—deep in the darkest, most hidden part of himself—that hers eclipsed his. He could charm his way into any woman's bed, play polo and golf at near-professional levels and speed-read a contract while dissecting a complicated financial statement.

But showing someone your wounds, revealing the bruises on your soul, took strength he didn't possess. Facing the past, wrestling with its jagged edges instead of locking it away in an unreachable vault, took a fortitude he could only admire from a distance. When it came to emotions, he was broken. Stunted. Incapable of anything more profound than surface-level banter. They said you learned how to love from the environment you grew up in, and while he'd witnessed the love his father bestowed on Alex, there'd been none left over for him. He'd received so little affection and love, he had no concept of how the process worked. To understand meant acknowledging he was unloved, and for most of his life that was too hard to do. He'd fallen into the self-protecting habit of dismissing it as being inconsequential and unneeded. As a result, feelings terrified him, and this woman, with her tears and her unbearable vulnerability, utterly dismantled him.

He tried to form words—words to tell her she was remarkable, that her courage left him in awe—but they stuck in his throat. They were too big, too tangled, too dangerous. They wouldn't come out. So he did the only thing he knew how to do: He retreated. He pulled back, slammed down his emotional shutters and wrapped himself in the cold, impenetrable roll cage that had always protected him. But because he needed to say something, anything, he retreated to where he felt comfortable. 'You should focus on work,' he said, wincing at his too-flat voice. 'You're great at what you do, and it's a good place to...' How to say this without revealing too much? '...lose yourself.'

She tipped her head, her eyes huge in her face. 'Is that what you do, Tazio?'

He couldn't admit that, couldn't widen that crack in his psyche. Not even with her, the woman who'd burrowed deeper under his skin than anyone else. He had to keep some distance, stay emotionally safe. Keep those feelings controlled and contained. 'We have so much to do, and little time to do it in. Let's get back to work.'

When hurt flickered in her eyes, he knew she'd been expecting a hug, some affection, maybe even for him to tell her that he was happy to see her. But he couldn't touch her, not now. If he did, his control would shatter and he'd expose how much he'd missed her, that he wanted her, would show her every inch of his emotional underbelly. Vulnerability was never acceptable.

Disappointment, stark and cutting, slashed through her eyes and across her face, a hot blade through butter.

They said he was an insensitive bastard. Cold. Unfeeling. Selfish. He hated labels and fought against being shoved into a box. But as he stood there, watching the light in her eyes dim, he knew the press, and the world, had him pegged.

CHAPTER TEN

IN THE DE ROSSI conference room at the Imola track, her back to the track, Millie pushed her laptop away and tried to stretch away the stress of the long day. Yesterday and the day before had hurtled past in a blur of chaos—exactly what she'd come to expect from the build-up to race-day. Taz had been busier than normal, his days taken up with race business, his nights with sponsor dinners, and he'd slipped into the bed they shared after she was asleep and quietly left before she was awake.

When they were together on the track, he occasionally wrapped his arm around her waist, dropped a kiss in her hair. But because people were always around when he was being affectionate, she never knew if it was to promote their supposed romance or if he was being genuinely affectionate.

He'd been surprisingly understanding about her absence from the track the other day—she'd expected a harsh scolding because Taz De Rossi did not appreciate his people not doing their jobs to his exacting standards!—and his saying she was doing a great job as his PR person both warmed and floored her. Again, compliments about work performance from him were hard to earn and exceedingly rare.

Millie sighed. They were both exceptionally busy and currently run off their feet and had little time to spend together. Conversations, mainly work-based, were rushed, and while they kept up their fake relationship in public and shared a bed at night, they hadn't connected on a personal level lately. Sure, their days were long and chaotic, but she couldn't help thinking Taz was avoiding her.

Since meeting up again, there had been fleeting moments of…oh, it was so hard to define! A glance. A hesitation. Heat that was quickly banked, a tiny spark of tenderness quickly smothered. He looked, only to her, like a man grappling with something he couldn't control, like he'd pulled the pin on a grenade and now didn't know where to throw it.

Her phone buzzed, and Millie frowned when she saw a message on the De Rossi employees group chat. Taz wanted the entire team to congregate on the track outside the De Rossi pit stop in five minutes. Millie raised her eyebrows. It was the end of the day, and everyone was tired. Why was Taz calling a team meeting now?

Millie made her way down to the track and joined her unusually sombre colleagues, a little confused at the unusual summons.

Taz, dressed in a dark suit with an open-necked white shirt, pushed his way through the crowd to her. He held a massive bouquet of white lilies and roses, which he pushed into her hands. Then, he took her hand in his, linking their fingers. Drivers and crew members from the other teams joined the De Rossi team.

Taz cleared his throat, and the crowd quietened. 'Millie James is Ben Brennan's cousin, and ten years ago, Ben lost his life on this very track.' He looked down at her. 'We are all here to remember Ben, Millie. Let's go, sweetheart,' he softly murmured, his deep voice surprisingly tender.

It took Millie a few beats for her to realise that Taz had arranged a memorial service for Ben, a way for her to commemorate his death and for his colleagues in the racing world to pay their respects to one of their own. And in doing so, he confirmed every instinct she'd had about him: that Taz was far better than the man he pretended to be. Hand in hand, they began a slow, deliberate walk onto the track. Behind them, the crowd followed—drivers, mechanics, managers, and others—moving quietly. The kaleidoscope of uniforms blended, team loyalties forgotten, united in paying tribute to one of their own. A wave of gratitude rolled through her. Taz wasn't just giving her a way to honour Ben, he was honouring her grief, her memories and her love for her cousin in a way that spoke louder than words ever could.

He'd used all his power and influence to create a moment she would carry with her forever. And for the first time in weeks, Millie felt as though she could finally begin to let go. Tears spilt freely down her cheeks. She clung to Taz's hand, his steady grip anchoring her as they walked. After several minutes, he guided her to the side of the track, his hand firm on her waist.

'This is where it happened,' he murmured, his voice low. 'This is where Ben crashed, Millie.'

She nodded, her throat tight with emotion. Dropping to her knees, she placed the bouquet on the edge of the track, her fingers brushing the cool asphalt. Her voice was barely a whisper, but she spoke anyway, hoping that somehow Ben could hear her.

'Ben, I miss you. So much. I wish I'd spent more time with you, that I'd seen you more. I'm sorry.'

On her haunches, she stared at the bouquet, grateful that Taz's big body formed a barrier between her and the crowd behind her. 'I'm trying to be better, Ben, and I'm slowly making sense of my life and my place in the world… I really hope you're proud of me, Ben,' she added, her tears flowing unchecked.

At the same time Taz's big hand came to rest on her shoulder, steadying and grounding her, Ben's voice rolled through her. *There wasn't a day I wasn't, Mils.*

For a fleeting moment, she thought she felt his presence—a breath of wind, his laughter dancing on the air. Then a deep voice rose behind her, singing the first line of 'Amazing Grace'.

Millie's composure shattered. Kneeling on the track with Taz behind her, shielding her, she sobbed for everything she'd lost: for the cousin who'd been like a brother, for the girl she used to be and for the woman she was struggling to become.

Hours later, comprehensively exhausted, Taz stood in the passage outside his hotel suite and rested his hand on the door. It had been a long and tough day in a series of long and tough days, and he was shattered. He was used to working hard, but organising Ben's memorial service had taken more effort than anybody—especially Millie—knew. Getting permission from the stewards to walk the track as a huge group, just a day before the time trials, had taken some persuading—the track was looked after like a newborn baby—and when that was done, he'd contacted the other teams and rallied support for the memorial. He hadn't wanted to raise her hopes in case he couldn't pull it off, so keeping it from Millie had been difficult. Apparently, he no longer liked hiding things from her. His thoughts, emotions, what he was thinking and doing.

And there was the root of his dilemma. He wanted to both protect himself and to deepen his connection to Millie. Wanted to keep his distance yet also know her inside out. While trying to run a multibillion-dollar company, manage his team and promote his charity work, he was consistently battered by conflicting emotions, desires and needs.

God, he was a mess. And he didn't like it. But he didn't—couldn't—regret arranging Ben's memorial service. He had done it partly as an apology for not immediately understanding why she couldn't face being at the track the day she arrived in Italy, and partly because he remembered Millie saying she wanted to visit the place where Ben died. Mostly because he suspected she needed to reconnect, even if it was through death, with her cousin. Bottom line: Millie'd needed it, so he'd stepped up and made it happen.

He couldn't stay out here, so Taz opened the door and stepped into the room. Millie sat on the bed, looking frail and played-out, emotionally whipped. Resisting the urge to scoop her up and cuddle her—he wasn't a cuddler!—he stayed by the door, keeping his restless hands in his trouser pockets.

'You need to eat, Millie,' he stated, his voice rough.

'I can't,' she replied. She lifted her shoulders and let them drop. Her huge, emotion-drenched eyes met his. 'How can I eat when words are bubbling inside me, when I have so much gratitude that needs to be expressed?'

He didn't want her thanks, couldn't handle her gratitude. It was too much. There were too many emotions swirling around, and he felt battered from all sides.

As per normal, he found words and conversation difficult and struggled to find the right response. 'Words aren't what I need, Mils.'

Moving toward him, she placed her hands flat against his chest, stood on her toes and placed her lips on his rough-with-stubble cheek. She stayed there for a long time—a minute or a decade? Who knew?—and when she finally returned to her feet, her eyes slammed into his, and he tumbled into a field of African violets…a lot of blue, hints of purple.

'What do you need, Taz?'

'I need you, Millie,' he whispered. God, he prayed she didn't ask him how or why or to explain that statement any further.

'You do?'

In so many ways he couldn't express. 'Will you stay with me tonight?'

'Yes.'

Millie's arms wrapped around his waist, handing him a hug he didn't know he needed. She was the one who'd cried today, who'd weathered an emotional storm, but now he was the one absorbing her warmth, sucking in her quiet strength. She recharged his batteries and refilled his well. Taz buried his nose in her fragrant hair as panic barrelled through him. What was happening to him and, more importantly, how on earth was he going to find the distance he knew he very badly needed?

After a night spent in Taz's arms—with comfort morphing into blistering sex—Millie woke feeling steadier. Not completely herself, but the grief-tinged panic seemed to have receded. She could go to the track today. Watching the race itself might be too much—she'd already decided she'd retreat to Taz's trailer if necessary—but she'd said her goodbyes to Ben yesterday. Now it was time to do her job.

The Italian sun warmed the hotel patio, and the lush gardens surrounding them buzzed with life. Millie poured fresh coffee into their cups, enjoying the quiet intimacy of the al fresco breakfast. Across the table, Taz looked distracted, his dark brows pulled together. He hummed with energy, and she knew today would be hard for him. For a man who thrived in the heat of competition, who craved control, being sidelined was agonising.

'I don't think you realise how touched I am by what you did yesterday,' she quietly said. 'I'm so grateful, Taz.'

'You thanked me last night, Millie,' he said, reaching for his coffee.

He was so comfortable basking in track victories and in front of cameras and doing deals, but he frowned and shifted in his seat when he was praised for being sweet and sensitive. Millie resisted the urge to say more, hoping Taz knew the depth of her gratitude.

Ben's memorial ceremony, and Taz's role in organising it, had made headline news this morning. Taz had been enjoying some good press for a while now, but this was the kind of story the media loved—a touching blend of tragedy and hope—but Millie knew Taz hadn't done it for the cameras. He'd done it for her.

This man, so tough and impenetrable, could also be tender and infuriatingly thoughtful when he chose to be.

He was an enigma wrapped up in a puzzle guarded by layers of computer code. Unhackable.

She bit into a strawberry, watching him. 'Did you have a big funeral for Alex?'

His hand tightened around his fork, his jaw going rigid. Millie winced internally. Wrong question. But she pressed on, hoping for a response. Any response. 'It's so strange and awful that two De Rossi drivers died so young. What was Alex like?'

For a moment, she thought he might answer, but then he replied, his voice colder and unexpectedly clipped. 'Look him up online.'

Her stomach sank. She recognised the tone: His walls were up, the subject closed. But she couldn't let it go. Not entirely.

'I don't want the internet's version of Alex. I want *your* version, Taz.' She leaned forward, cradling her coffee cup. 'What was he like as your brother? I could tell you a thousand little things about Ben—how he cried during animated movies or hated needles. That he loved shoving asparagus stalks up his nose to make me laugh. It's the stupid things, the little things, that made him *him*.'

'What's with the interrogation, Millie? We're sleeping together, not sharing our deepest secrets.'

His words hit her like a slap, but she didn't flinch. She knew his sharpness masked pain, that he lashed out when he felt cornered. 'I'm trying to have a conversation with you, Tazio, about your brother. This is what people do.'

He tossed his serviette onto the table and released a huff of annoyance. 'I don't,' he snapped.

She should back off, but she had come this far, she might as well see it through. Yesterday had been cathartic for her, and she wanted Taz to feel the same peace. Oh, she still didn't know who exactly she was or where she was going, but she wasn't nearly as lost as she was before.

She felt less emotional, and some of her ghosts had been laid to rest. She wanted Taz to feel of little of the relief she did. Was that so wrong?

'Alex is someone to be proud of, to be celebrated,' Millie gently stated. 'He was a good guy, so why don't you talk about him? He was your big brother and part of your life. And while we're on the subject, why don't you talk about your dad?'

'Millie, I have a busy day ahead of me, and I don't want it to begin with a fight.'

Millie wrinkled her nose. 'I don't want to fight either. I'm trying to have a conversation with you.'

'We can talk about anyone or anything *but* Alex—or my dad,' Taz quickly added.

'Why is everything that matters off-limits with you?' Millie asked, keeping her tone gentle.

Taz's chair scraped against the stone as he stood abruptly, his movements sharp with tension. 'You don't have the first clue about Alex. Or my father. And I don't owe you any explanations.'

She looked up at him, her heart twisting. 'I agree you don't owe me anything, Taz. But holding all this in—it's only hurting you.'

His laugh was humourless, the sound hollow. 'Stay out of my head, Millie.'

And with that, he walked away, leaving her alone on the sunlit patio. As she watched his broad back retreat, she felt something shift between them—a crack widening, impossible to ignore.

* * *

When Millie arrived at the Autodromo Internazionale Enzo e Dino Ferrari later that day, she was alone. After storming off, Taz had left the hotel without speaking to her again, forcing her to call an intern to collect her, a humiliation to go along with her shredded nerves.

It was race-day, and her earlier courage had dissolved like water droplets on a hot pavement. Now she was holding herself together with fine, fraying threads of mental superglue. One hour until the race. She glanced at her watch, the ticking hands a constant countdown. Coffee was out, but a cup of chamomile and ginger tea might soothe her jangling nerves, and she'd swallow a few of the homoeopathic anxiety pills she kept tucked in her bag.

Her rational brain told her she was being absurd. What had happened ten years ago was a freak accident and statistically impossible to repeat. But rationalisations didn't quiet her anxiety. It wasn't only the track or the memories, it was the coming together of too many emotions—her deepening feelings for Taz, her lack of sleep and her inability to understand how they could veer from passion to tension to frustration and back again in a matter of minutes.

Millie stepped into the hospitality suite grateful it was empty. The muffled roar of the crowd drifted through the window, and Millie wondered what had caught their attention. Refusing to look out the window, she rubbed her burning eyes.

She missed Ben. He should've been here. Even if he wasn't racing, he'd be at the centre of it all—bantering with the pit crew, trading insults with the mechanics, laughing with the support staff. Ben had been so vibrant, so present. He'd lived in the moment, someone who loved what he did with every fibre of his being.

Millie wanted to be that kind of person. She loved the work she was doing for Taz and was constantly surprised by how good she was at it. Her knack for finding the heart of a problem, for peeling back layers to reveal a story that resonated, had transformed Taz in the eyes of the press. He was no longer just a volatile, selfish hothead—though, admittedly, he still was to some degree. Over the past few weeks, she'd reframed him, and now he was viewed as a burdened team owner and driver, the man who carried the weight of the De Rossi legacy on his shoulders.

And she hadn't spun lies to make it happen. Everything she'd said about Taz was true. He bore the crushing responsibility of his team, his employees, his sponsors' expectations—and his unrelenting ambition. The weight would be staggering for anyone, but for Taz? It seemed to harden his defences, fortifying his sharp edges and impenetrable walls.

His inability to discuss Alex, to allow her to peek behind his emotional walls, was deeply frustrating and a little hurtful. His rejection stung, but she'd noticed the storm raging inside him. There was so much she didn't know—so much he'd never let her see. Unless he chose to let her in, they would never be more than what they were now: unexpected flashes of tenderness, stolen moments in bed, tethered by nothing but desire.

Why did she want more?

Because something in Taz De Rossi called to her. Beneath the arrogance and the fire, she'd glimpsed a man who was deeply lonely, profoundly isolated. And, yes, he could be brutal and demanding, but there was also kindness in him, flashes of goodness that made her chest ache. He was infuriatingly complicated. He was many things at different times, and trying to make sense of Taz De Rossi was like trying to staple mist to a wall.

Her current exhaustion made her feel shaky and weak, and it amplified everything—her hurt, her anger, her impossible attraction to a man who was far too dangerous. When she felt steadier, when she was stronger, she'd untangle her emotions and decide what, if anything, they meant.

But she doubted they'd fade or would shrink to manageable levels, and suspected she was already in too deep. And she didn't think she could swim her way out.

In the hallway, Taz stopped dead as the door to the hospitality suite clicked shut behind Millie, the loud snick reverberating down the empty passage.

He tipped his head back, eyes fixed on the ceiling, looking for a way to ease the storm raging inside him. Today was not going to plan. Not even close. Every cell in his body ached to be on the track, clad in his De Rossi colours, listening to the roar of his car's engine, navigating the track's twists and turns. He knew what he was doing on the track.

He was wasting time and points, hampered and sidelined by his damned cast. Frustration dug its nails into his soul as the ugly combination of rage and helplessness swamped him. And because the universe seemed to delight in screwing with him, he'd taken out his anger on Millie earlier. She hadn't deserved it—but her simple questions about his brother and father had been enough to set him off. It was a topic he'd deflected a thousand times before, so why had it pierced through his shell this time? Why had *she*?

Taz braced a hand against the wall and let his forehead rest against it, his teeth grinding.

Millie was a problem he hadn't anticipated. He'd always compartmentalised his life—emotions in one box, sex in another and racing in a sacred safe all its own. But Millie had smashed some of those boxes, blurring the perfect lines he'd spent years drawing. She was a walking contradiction: infuriating and fascinating, soothing and incendiary. She'd painted his black-and-white world with wild streaks of vibrant colour.

He hated it.

He wanted more.

Taz groaned and banged his cast against the wall, shaking his head to clear it. He'd completed the bulk of the charity events he'd committed to—all with Millie at his side—and only had the ball in Monaco to attend. In three weeks, he'd be racing again, and life would return to being predictable, and he could focus on winning the championship. Proving, once and for all, that he was the best driver in his family, the greatest De Rossi to ever race.

The thought left him hollow.

Instead of relief, he felt…lost.

His jaw tightened. *Enough.* If he was going to survive the next three weeks, he needed to fix the mess he'd made with Millie. Lashing out at her had been cowardly. He hated cowardice; it was wholly unacceptable.

Steeling himself, he slipped into the hospitality suite, locking the door behind him. Millie turned at the sound, her brows arching, her expression cool.

Her outfit was simple—black jeans, a De Rossi team shirt, and high-tops—but Taz's pulse kicked up. Like two thousand other employees, she wore his name, but at seeing his name above her heart, something primal and possessive unfurled in his chest. He shoved the thought down, then stomped on it.

'Millie,' he began, his voice low, careful.

She sipped from her mug, her gaze steady, unwavering. She wasn't going to make this easy for him.

Good. He didn't deserve easy.

'I was out of line this morning,' he said, his words clipped but honest. 'You didn't deserve that. I shouldn't have—'

'Snapped? Stormed off?' she supplied.

'Exactly,' he admitted, forcing himself to meet her eyes. 'Sorry.'

The tension in her shoulders remained. 'Apologies aren't your strong suit, are they, Taz?' she said, her voice softer now but no less firm.

'No,' he confessed. 'But I'm learning.'

Her lips twitched, almost, but she caught herself, the flash of amusement replaced by wariness.

'Why did you snap at me?' she asked, crossing her arms, her vulnerability shielded behind her resolve.

Because you matter too much. Because you see through the masks I've worn for years, and I don't like it. He didn't say that, of course. Instead he shrugged, his hands slipping into his pockets. She studied him for a moment, her gaze piercing, and Taz realised he was holding his breath.

Finally, she sighed, setting her cup on the counter. 'You're a mess, Taz De Rossi,' she muttered, but there was no heat in her words.

His lips quirked. 'I've been called worse.'

Her mouth softened, and for the first time all day, he felt the knot in his chest loosen. He wasn't out of the woods, not by a long shot, but at least he wasn't wandering in the dark alone.

Tired, he walked over to the fridge, pulled out a bottle of water and cracked the top.

'You're way too nice, Mils,' he said, resting the bottle on his forehead. He rolled it across his forehead, hoping the cool plastic would ease his headache. Words he didn't expect to utter left his mouth. 'Remember I asked you whether Ben had said anything to you about Alex?'

What was he doing? Why was he reopening this door, edging it open a crack? 'We didn't speak about Alex, Taz,' Millie replied. 'Our conversations didn't include a lot of racing talk. What I knew about Alex was what I read online.'

Drivers were normally chatty, sometimes gossipy, guys. Did Ben not talk about Alex because he knew who he really was, and how he spent his free time, when he wasn't with Meredith or out in public? Had Ben known about the drugs and the young girls? If he did, why didn't he say anything?

As soon as the thought formed, he had his answer. Because nobody would've believed him. Alex was the favourite son of the team's owner. If he'd criticised Alex, Ben would've sounded like he was whining or making trouble and it was a case of sour grapes.

There was no universe in which Ben could criticise Alex and come out with his good reputation intact.

He lifted the water bottle, drank half its contents and forced his eyes to meet Millie's. He'd tell her the bare minimum, enough for her to understand. 'I don't talk about Alex because…' Shit, this was hard.

He sighed, swallowed and sighed again. 'Alex wasn't the person everyone thought he was.'

She looked confused, as he knew she would. 'What do you mean?'

'That's all I can say.' There was so much more, but those few words felt like someone had poured acid down his throat.

Millie stood, put her cup on the table and folded her arms.

'Can you give me a little more?' she asked.

Didn't she realise that she'd got more from him than anyone since the night Alex died? That those few halting words needed more courage than barrelling down an endless salt pan in a car made for speed and not safety? Conversations like these were far more dangerous than anything the racing world could throw at him.

Taz dragged his shaking hand over his jaw, his self-assurance in tatters. But instead of probing for answers or demanding more, Millie did something that completely disarmed him. She walked over, placed both hands on his chest and rested her forehead on his sternum. Her arms slipped around his waist in a tight, wordless hug. No ulterior motive. No agenda. Just quiet, undemanding comfort.

Taz froze, utterly blindsided. Like last night, her embrace wasn't sexual or flirtatious—it was *human*. And yet his knees wobbled like he'd walked away from a death-defying crash. He couldn't remember the last time someone had offered him solace without expecting something in return. Before his mother died, perhaps? But those memories were buried under decades of grief and loss, hazy with time.

Millie pulled back, tilting her head to meet his gaze, her eyes were soft with understanding. Her fingertips brushed his jaw in a feather-light caress.

'It must be exhausting always being compared to him,' she said, her voice a low murmur. 'I'm so sorry, Taz.'

Her words pierced his armour and burned his skin. Taz blinked hard, desperate to banish the burning in his eyes. He couldn't lose it, not here, not now. Emotion was self-indulgent and useless, a luxury he'd discarded in his teens. So why was it so damned difficult to push her away? To create the distance he knew he needed?

A knock broke the spell he was under, a welcome distraction. It jolted him back to the present, and when the door-handle rattled, he remembered he'd locked it. Grateful for the interruption, he strode to the door, unlocked it and yanked it open.

The intern standing in the hallway flinched at his scowl. 'Uh… Mr De Rossi, they're waiting for you in the briefing room,' the young man stammered.

Taz nodded curtly, his jaw tight. 'I'll be there in a minute.'

When the intern didn't turn and flee, Taz's scowl deepened. 'Is there something else?'

The kid took a step back. 'Uh… Mr De Rossi…uh… the car is here.'

'The car?'

'You ordered a car to take Ms James back to the hotel, sir. It's waiting for her.'

Right. *That*. He'd forgotten that he wanted Millie away from the race this afternoon. Yesterday's impromptu memorial service had been rough on her, and he suspected she was still dealing with the emotional storm. There were other races she would attend, but there was nothing she needed to do this afternoon. She did not need to watch the race at the track where Ben died.

'Give us a minute,' Taz told the kid and shut the door. Rubbing the back of his neck, he walked over to where Millie stood, clearly confused.

He pushed a long tendril behind her ear and hooked it behind her ear. 'Go home, Millie. You don't need to be here.'

She shook her head, her stubborn chin lifting. 'I can't, Taz. I have work to do.'

No, she didn't. Not today. 'There's nothing that can't wait until tomorrow, and I promise not to cause a PR disaster between now and then.' He cupped her face, and she pushed her soft cheek into his palm. 'I don't want you watching the race. I don't want your imagination working overtime, for you to think about what happened to Ben. Go back to the hotel, swim. Fall asleep in the shade on a lounger by the pool. Think about anything but this race.'

Her stunning eyes filled with tears, and a few ran down her cheek. Her hand covered his and she nodded, her bottom lip trembling. 'Thank you,' she said, sniffing hard. 'I didn't know how to watch the race and not watch the race, if you know what I mean.'

He wrapped his arm around her shoulder and roughly pulled her into him, thinking how well she fit into his much bigger body, like a puzzle piece he never knew was missing. He turned his head to kiss the top of hers. Looking over her shoulder, he caught a glimpse of his watch-face and grimaced at the time. He needed to be down in the pit, at the coalface. 'Mils…'

She pulled back and bobbed her head. 'You need to get going,' she stated, quickly wiping away her tears. 'Of course you do.'

'I'll walk you to the car.' He really shouldn't. He was needed elsewhere, but this was…well, this was Millie.

She sent him a look of reproach, the sting removed by her soft smile. 'And every reporter will wonder why I'm leaving and whether we've fought, whether I'm not feeling well, whether—' she slapped her hands to her face and rolled her eyes '—I'm pregnant! No, let's avoid the drama, and I'll sneak out quietly.'

He didn't like it. 'Are you sure?'

Millie nodded. 'I need a couple of minutes to get my stuff, so you go on.' He didn't move, and Millie released a quick huff. 'I promise you that I'm not going to stay here and work, Taz. I *will* go back to the hotel.'

She was the only person ever who could even remotely read his mind. And because he saw the sincerity in her eyes, he nodded, then swiped his mouth across hers. 'Have a good afternoon.'

She smiled. 'See you later?' she asked.

He nodded. 'I'm not sure when I'll be back.' But he'd be with her as soon as he could. He didn't know where they were going or how they'd pan out, so he intended to spend all the time he could with her.

CHAPTER ELEVEN

Monaco

MILLIE AND TAZ left Italy and arrived in Monaco the day after the race at Imola. Instead of flying, Taz bundled her into what she thought was a Bugatti (her knowledge about cars was abysmal) and they drove from Imola to Monaco. As they entered the heart of Monaco six hours later, Millie made a concerted effort to keep her excitement from showing on her face. It was the week leading up to the Grand Prix, and the city buzzed with anticipation and energy. The bright blue Mediterranean shimmered under the sun, and the luxury yachts in the harbour gleamed.

Locals and tourists alike were caught up in the excitement. Cafés were crowded and lively conversation punctuated the warm air. High heels clicked against the cobblestone streets. The city was a mix of sophistication and chaos, a place where the race was as much a reason for the world's rich and beautiful to gather as it was a sporting spectacle. Monaco gleamed. And preened.

Millie noticed people pointing their phones at them and heard the buzz of excitement when gearheads and Formula One fans recognised Taz. They stopped at a traffic light, and the car was quickly surrounded by fans and paparazzi. Taz was mobbed by requests for selfies and autographs.

Taz leaned across to her, and on the pretence of kissing her cheek, murmured in her ear. 'I've got to get you and this car off the street, or else we're going to be mobbed.'

Millie nodded her agreement, and when the light turned green Taz revved the engine and inched forward. The crowd parted and they roared away, and a few blocks later reached their hotel.

Because Taz was Taz and a global sensation, they were whisked up to his penthouse suite with a minimum of fuss. The panoramic views of the Mediterranean and the iconic skyline immediately captured Millie's attention. The penthouse was extensive, open and airy, its furnishings sleek and modern. An infinity pool ran the length of the suite, and Millie didn't need to explore to know that it would include a huge bedroom with an oversize bed, a bathroom that could accommodate thirty people and, possibly, a private gym.

Millie stretched, her eyes on the breath-stealing view. It was after two, and since they'd stopped for lunch along the way, they needed to get some work done today. She'd lost time yesterday, and her to-do list was as long as the circuit snaking through the city.

'Are you going to head down to the track?' she asked Taz, who'd walked over to stand next to her. Instead of looking at the view, his eyes were on her face. 'Why are you looking at me like that?' she asked, a little self-conscious at his intense stare. 'Why aren't you admiring the view? It's stunning.'

'Because you are far more interesting,' he told her, his voice becoming a little deeper, a tad richer. Gruffer.

'I have an appointment with the team doctor in an hour, and the stylist is coming here with a selection of dresses for you to wear to the ball tomorrow night.'

It was the last event she'd agreed to attend as his fake girlfriend, and the most high-profile. Millie wrinkled her nose. 'Why can't he choose one? I've got so much to do,' she complained.

'You need to choose.' Taz placed his hand on her hip and pulled her closer. 'But since we both have an hour…'

His lips hit the spot on her neck where she was most sensitive, and she could feel him growing harder against her stomach. She didn't have time for this, she had about a hundred emails she needed to respond to and calls to return. But Taz's lips on her skin felt like heaven, and when he moved his mouth up her neck, across her jaw and onto hers, she sighed. She'd work harder later. Making love to Taz was all that was important right now…

'Millie…'

His mouth claimed hers with unapologetic hunger, bypassing tenderness and heading straight into a kiss that was ferocious, desperate. His tongue invaded, retreated, then plunged back in, a reckless rhythm that left her breathless. He was a fine wine and dark chocolate, a jolt of adrenaline and a dizzying fall. Millie melted into his heat, craving more than his kisses.

She pressed her hips into his, her sigh mingling with his low groan. Yes. More. Of everything he could give her. Work could wait.

But Taz stepped back, his hands the only tether between them as they traced the line of her jaw, his expression fierce yet controlled. 'Why did you stop?' The question slipped out before she realised she'd spoken.

His voice was rough, strained. 'Because I don't want it to be over too fast. I want more for you than fast.'

Her laugh was breathy, laced with need. 'I don't mind fast.'

Taz shook his head, the corner of his mouth quirking into a wicked smile. 'Not this time, Mils.'

His shortening her name softened her. It made her feel claimed and cherished. Dangerous thoughts. This wasn't love—it *couldn't* be. But when he bent and swept her into his arms, carrying her with effortless strength, the lines between what was possible and what was not, between sex and love, blurred.

In the bedroom, decorated in soft sea-greens and whites, he set her down in front of a tall, free-standing mirror. Moving to stand behind her, with a sexy combination of need and simmering restraint, he met her eyes in the glass. His hands came to rest on her shoulders, his touch scorching her skin through the fabric of her shirt.

'Your only job is to watch me,' he commanded softly, his voice like smoke and silk.

With aching slowness, from behind her he undid the buttons of her shirt, revealing her skin inch by inch. His hands traced her collarbone and slid the fabric from her arms, and she shivered as her lace bra came into view. He kissed the curve of her neck, cupped her breasts and kneaded them with reverence and complete focus. Her nipples pebbled under his touch, and her breath caught.

'Look at yourself,' he murmured, voice roughened by desire. 'See how beautiful you are. You're luscious, Millie. Bold and bright.'

'No, I'm just—'

'Just gorgeous, and so sexy you make me dizzy,' he

muttered, in his sex-and-sandpaper voice. He shook her lightly. 'Look at yourself. See what I see.'

Her reflection in the mirror shocked her. A sexy woman, one she barely recognised, stared back at her with flushed cheeks and eyes dark with desire. She was luminous and vibrant. Someone who could, and should, be confident in her own skin, in what she could offer the world. In what she could offer *him*. Maybe it was time to start seeing herself differently, to break the habit of putting herself down.

Taz's hands left her breasts to unclasp her bra, the straps falling away like ribbons, baring her completely.

Her breath hitched as he slid a hand beneath the waistband of her shorts, the other hand caressing her spine. 'God, Millie,' he rasped, voice hoarse with need. 'You're stunning. I can't wait to be inside you.'

Swept away with the raw intensity in his voice, her inhibitions dissolved. Millie hastily shed her clothes and stood between him and the mirror, clothed in nothing but heat and hunger. Taz moved to kneel, his shoulders pushing her thighs apart, and she gasped. Too much. Too intimate.

'Trust me,' he whispered.

She did. He kissed her there, where no one but him had kissed her, with such tenderness, such raw intensity. Sparkling sensations rolled over her, pulling her under, scattering her thoughts like wedding confetti. His mouth painted magic over her skin, his fingers teased, and when her climax hit, it was an obliteration, a release that left her trembling and weightless. Transformed.

Taz pulled back, his face flushed, his chest heaving

as he gazed at her with reverent satisfaction, pleased by her response, utterly confident in his skill.

He stood, a towering figure of strength and passion, and she held out her hand, lacing her fingers with his. 'Now, Taz,' she whispered. 'Make love to me.'

And when he kissed her again, slow and consuming, Millie wondered if this was love, if Taz was the man she'd hand her heart to. What would he do with it if she did?

Would he cherish it or crush it?

But as long as he kept kissing her like this, she didn't really care.

CHAPTER TWELVE

THE NEXT EVENING, Taz stood by the edge of the infinity pool, the cool night air brushing against his bare chest. With only a towel wrapped around his hips, he scowled at the Mediterranean Sea, its surface unnervingly still.

He should've been enjoying shower sex with Millie, and the taste of her mouth still lingered on his lips, the heat of her body pressed against his. Instead, his jaw was tight, and his hands flexed at his sides as he relived the moment that had shattered their intimacy.

The insistent, strident ringing of his phone.

He'd heard it even through the rush of water in the power shower, but he'd ignored it. Who cared about the rest of the world when Millie was naked in his arms? His soapy hands had been sliding over her curves, her skin slick and warm beneath his touch, when the braying ringing broke the moment.

Reluctantly, he'd stepped out of the shower, water dripping off him as he snatched up the towel and wrapped it around his waist. He'd reached for the phone, already annoyed, and that was when his afternoon rapidly slid downhill.

'What the *hell* do you mean that it's been delayed?'

He checked the knot of his towel and rested his forearms on the railing, taking in his logistics manager's report. Essentially, a large shipment of car parts, including crucial tyres, specialised tools and performance equipment, had been caught up in a blockade by striking truck drivers in France and its arrival would be delayed by several days. Taz gripped the bridge of his nose. The equipment was needed by his mechanical team so they could start fine-tuning the car set-up and getting it ready for the demanding street circuit.

'With the strike still ongoing, no one can tell me when the backlog will begin to move.'

Taz thought fast. They had duplicates of everything they needed at the De Rossi headquarters and research centre in the UK. He gave his manager the go-ahead to hire a cargo plane and ordered him to move heaven and earth to get the parts to Monaco as soon as humanly possible.

Shit. He killed the call and banged the edge of his palm against the railing, frustrated and annoyed.

Dealing with delays wasn't something new, it was part of the logistical circus that came with moving a huge F1 team from one glittering city to another, but tonight Taz felt rattled. The kind of rattled he hadn't felt in years. Control was his oxygen. He thrived on it, needed it, but lately? It was slipping through his fingers, slick and treacherous like oil on a wet track.

Since Shanghai, his life had become an impossible tightrope walk above a thousand-foot chasm without safety ropes. So much changed—and quickly. He'd lost his temper, been sidelined by injury, acquired a fake girlfriend and somehow found a real lover. And yesterday, sitting in his doctor's office, they'd finally cut away the cast on his hand.

'It's been five weeks, and you've healed well. Technically you could race,' his doctor cautiously told him, 'but I wouldn't recommend it.'

But Taz needed to be behind the wheel. Saturday couldn't come fast enough.

He'd kept the news to himself, unable to tell Millie, his race engineers or the team. The Taz he used to be would've already announced his triumphant return to the world he ruled, enjoying the attention and standing in the spotlight. But the man he was today, staring at the late-afternoon sun dipping under the horizon, was different. Over the past few weeks since he'd gotten closer to Millie, he felt like he'd become softer, more vulnerable, like some of his armour had fallen away. He didn't like feeling exposed.

He pushed his hand through his hair, wishing he could blow off the ball, but he was the guest of honour. It was yet another PR circus, designed to soften his image, make him a little more human, a little less controversial. But his idea of having Millie at his side had been a genius one. Sure, a nice girlfriend helped his image but, with her there, he was less impatient, a lot more tolerant, less abrasive. Nicer to be around.

All good things. But what wasn't good was that Millie knew Alex wasn't the saint everyone believed him to be. He'd given her no details, but if he did, he knew she'd understand and empathise. But telling her required an enormous amount of trust, more than he could give. If nobody but him knew of Alex's secret, then it was forever safe. If he told Millie everything about that night, he'd feel utterly vulnerable, exposed and completely dis-mantled. He'd regret that he'd told her and worry she'd let the information about Alex slip, and those initial niggles of worry would swell to full-blown anxiety.

The sound of soft footsteps pulled him from his thoughts, and Millie's cool hand settled on his bare back.

Her freshly washed hair tumbled over her shoulders in damp waves, catching the fading light. She wore a skimpy vest and a pair of soft cotton shorts, her bare feet silent on the stone tiles.

For a moment, the chaos quieted. The noise in his head dulled.

'Problem?' she asked.

He nodded and explained, enjoying her hand on his bare back. 'It sounds like you found a solution,' she stated. 'Now, what's really worrying you?'

How did she find the crack, the gap, in his carefully constructed emotional fence? When had she developed the ability to blow past his shields and look into the raw, unspoken, unacknowledged parts of him? Goddamn, he hated it.

Taz shrugged, the movement sharp and dismissive. But before he could move away, she gripped his wrist.

'Tazio.' Her using his full name was her way of chal-lenging him, saying that she wasn't going to be brushed off. He wanted to push her away, to keep her at arm's length, but couldn't.

Her eyes met his, as much inquisitive as sympathetic. 'Don't shut me out.'

He planted his feet, his back rigid, his chest tight. 'Why do you have to push?' he demanded.

Her fingers tightened ever so slightly on his arm. 'It

was a simple question, Taz. A way for me to remind you
that I'm here and ready to listen.'

The words hit him harder than they should have. Because they both knew she wasn't talking about the delayed
shipment or him racing on Saturday. She was talking
about all of it—the walls, the shields, the secrets buried
deep. She was offering him the one thing he'd never allowed anyone: the chance to be seen, truly seen, for everything he was.

Taz opened his mouth, then closed it, unsure what to
say. How did he explain that he was beyond fixing?

But he needed to regain lost ground, so he latched on
to an easy out.

He raked his hair off his forehead. 'What do you want
me to tell you? My standings in the championship are
slipping, my lead is eroding. My mechanics are anxious
because their parts aren't here, and that's stressful. I also
have to make nice at a ball when I should be working on
race strategy.'

'Why are you so determined to win a fourth championship? Is it because Alex didn't?'

So sharp. She saw too much, and as a person who'd
spent his entire life hiding his emotions, her ability to
peek over his walls terrified him.

'Partly.'

'Alex is dead, Taz. Nobody cares,' she stated, confused.
He couldn't deny it: The most he'd get when he beat Alex's
record would be a brief mention of his achievement by
sports journalists. But that wasn't the point. How could
he explain it was personal and precious, a way for him
to stand in front of the memory of his father, and say that
he mattered, he counted, that he was as worthy of space

and attention as Alex? That they'd been wrong to ignore and discount him?

'I wish you'd talk to me, Taz.'

Didn't she get it? In just a few weeks, he'd told her more than he'd shared with anyone over the course of his life. 'I rarely talk to anyone, and I never talk to anyone about Alex. Ever.' His voice was harsh and clipped, every word coated with regret. 'I can't trust anyone.'

Her face tightened, and he knew he'd hurt her, saw it in the way she blinked the pain away. But Millie being Millie, she didn't crumble. She held her ground. 'Are you worried I'll say something? Fine. I'll sign an NDA. If anything gets out, sue me for everything I have. I'll repay you the million plus interest.' Her voice was steady, but there was steel in it, a fierce edge that told him she wasn't bluffing. 'But you need to know this. I will *never* betray you.'

The words hit harder than he wanted to admit, slicing through the panic that had been twisting in his gut for what felt like forever. She wasn't the problem. He was. The unfamiliar feelings she raised in him, the feeling of becoming more vulnerable with every moment he spent with her, terrified him.

Panic twisted his gut.

'You're competing with a ghost, Taz.'

He couldn't do this anymore. He dragged his hand over his face, hoping to wipe the tension away. He needed to regain control of himself and the conversation—immediately. Before he could speak, Millie did him a favour and changed the subject. 'So are you going to race on Saturday?'

He looked down at his cast-free hand. 'How did you know?'

She scoffed and rolled her eyes. 'Your cast is off, your lead is slipping, and you want to get back on the track.'

She turned, and he let her go. Watching her walk back into the penthouse, he mused on how he'd once considered their relationship uncomplicated, black-and-white. A fake couple in public, lovers in private.

The one thing he couldn't control—the one thing that threatened everything he thought he knew—was that she might, genuinely, care for him. And that despite his best efforts, he cared for her too. He might even be close to falling for her.

And that was too big a risk.

Because if he let her in, really let her in, she'd be a car he couldn't chase down, a crash he couldn't avoid. Loving her—and losing her, because love never stayed—would tear him apart.

But, God, he wasn't sure that he had enough courage to let her go.

They walked into the ballroom of Le Château du Ciel hotel, and Millie glanced at Taz. He seemed unimpressed by the unfiltered decadence of the best ballroom in the superrich principality. The ceiling was a masterpiece handpainted with almost-naked gods and goddesses lounging on clouds, laughing down at the mortals beneath them. Impressive, oversize crystal chandeliers dripped from the frescoed ceiling, and the polished Italian marble floors gleamed like glass.

Mirrors on the walls were framed in intricate gold leaf. The floor-to-ceiling arched windows were outlined by velvet drapes in a deep, rich midnight blue. They were, in Millie's view, superfluous because the view of the city and Mediterranean beyond the balcony was incredible.

With her hand lodged in Taz's elbow, Millie looked around and noticed a piano sitting under a spotlight at the far end of the large room. A quartet played, but she couldn't hear any music above the chatter of the rich, famous and infamous. Waiters in white gloves glided through the crowd, offering crystal flutes of champagne and trays of hors d'oeuvres.

Millie caught their reflection in a mirror and cast a critical eye over her appearance. Her dress was deep purple, shot with silver. It hugged her in all the right places, its neckline dipping low enough to make it interesting, cinching at her waist before spilling into a dramatic skirt that showed a hint of her three-inch heels. Her makeup was understated, her hair pulled back into a smooth, sleek tail.

Taz in a tuxedo suited this ballroom like a sword did a scabbard. His classic black suit was exquisitely tailored, the sharp lines highlighting his broad shoulders and athletic build. The crisp white shirt was a stark contrast to his tanned face and neck, and his three-day dark stubble was a reminder to everyone that he was, despite his wealth, a rebel and a bad boy. He looked every inch the charming, untouchable, remote billionaire he was. Oh, his effortless, rakish smile was in place, but she could easily differentiate between Authentic Taz and Pretend Taz. His charm was frequently superficial, his urbanity a cloak he'd pulled on to fool the world.

Since their breakfast discussion in Italy about Alex, he'd been inching away, emotionally distancing himself. Oh, he was still a fantastic lover, devoted to her pleasure, but his conversation was less easy, his responses more measured and never impetuous. It was as if he was afraid to let something important or personal slip.

His retreat hurt more than Millie expected, and hearing the edge in his voice, something he probably wasn't even aware of, stung. His carefully constructed façade had solidified again, she could see it in the set of his jaw, the way his eyes quickly moved from hers when they spoke. His emotional walls were higher than before, and those flashes of vulnerability she'd seen in him were a thing of the past.

Was asking him about his brother such a big sin? Could he not trust that his secrets were safe with her? Her insecurities rushed back, hot and hard, punching and kicking in a relentless ambush. She didn't belong in this opulent ballroom and wasn't good enough to be hanging onto Taz's arm. She wasn't thin enough, pretty enough, vivacious or charming enough.

Recognising her spiralling thoughts, she locked her knees and pushed steel into her spine.

Stop.

Breathe.

Think.

Under her skirts, she stomped her foot, clad in its designer shoe. She loathed her self-doubt and cursed its return. *Remember how far you've come, Millie!* She'd managed to navigate this unfamiliar world, maybe not as effortlessly as her parents and Taz did, but she hadn't embarrassed herself. Nobody, not the press or her colleagues at De Rossi Racing, questioned whether she was good enough to be with Taz. They assumed she was. So why was she doubting herself? Was it Taz's inability or unwillingness to open up and talk to her that made her question herself and wonder if she was sufficiently strong, witty and smart to be his partner, to stand by his side?

It had been his choice not to open up; she'd done nothing wrong. Just like she wasn't defective or substandard because she felt uncomfortable with her parents' pursuit of publicity. Taz and her parents were responsible for their own choices, and she for hers.

While she'd never be a society hostess, she had come a long way, and balls, cocktail parties and red carpets didn't make her quake in her heels anymore. Professionally, in terms of her and Taz's agreement, she'd done her job. She'd rehabilitated his reputation and built it back up in the media after weeks of scandal and bad press. Taz was now seen in a more favourable light, and when he announced he was racing this weekend, the press would go wild. She'd already prepared the press releases, ready to go as soon as he gave her the green light. He'd be fine.

But would she?

Probably, eventually, but she'd have to live with a strange emptiness deep in her soul. She liked her work and enjoyed being good at it, but what she really wanted—what she craved—was simple: to hold Taz's full attention, to be the focus of it. She wanted to be the one person who mattered, apart from and beyond the reputation he was rebuilding or the races he was winning.

Yes, she wanted to stay in his world, but not for the flashing cameras, the extravagant cars or clothes or red carpets. She no longer needed to prove she was worthy, to her parents or to herself. She was, simply because she was Millie. No, her motivation to stick with it was simple: she wanted to be wherever Taz was.

But Taz didn't want what she did; he wasn't looking for anything permanent. He liked the thrill of a lover, but that was where it ended. He couldn't give her what she needed. Her choice was simple: She could either walk away or watch the man she was falling for, the man she loved, leave by degrees.

Either way, she'd end up alone…

'Millie, I asked whether you wanted another drink.'

Taz's annoyance cut through her reverie, and she jerked. 'Uh… I'm fine, thanks.'

Taz plucked her glass from her hand and placed it on the tray of a passing waiter. He raked his hand through his hair and dropped a low-pitched for-her-ears-only F-bomb.

'Problem?' she asked.

He sighed, and a muscle in his jaw ticked. He put his back to the room, and his expression morphed from geniality to annoyance. 'All this?' His gesture encompassed the glittering crowd, the music and the chattering crowd. 'It's a waste of time. I should be at the track, preparing.'

She pulled his jacket sleeve back and squinted at his Rolex. 'Give it another two hours and you can slip out,' Millie told him. She saw his stubborn face and sighed. 'You agreed to attend, Taz. Your presence and support are *important*.'

His mouth tightened. 'The only thing that matters is what happens on the track. Winning is everything.'

He was so single-minded, and now that he could resume racing, he'd reverted to being selfish about his time. His view had narrowed, and only racing held his interest. Many people, including her, had worked overtime to make this event happen. And the charities were going to get a very healthy injection of funds into their war chest.

But all the work they'd done, all the money they'd raised, meant nothing to Taz.

Had he ever seen the real value in aligning himself with the charities, beyond rehabilitating his reputation and winning the championship? Had she fooled herself into thinking he was a better man than he was?

And if he couldn't even value this event, he certainly didn't value her and the work she'd put in on his behalf. Everything, every atom of his being, was focused on and directed at being a four-time championship winner. There was no space in his life for her.

Millie's breath caught in her throat, and her heart wanted to slink out of her chest. She was nothing more than a brief blip in his world of cars and fame and championship glory.

But she was too far in. She'd fallen too hard, too fast and too deep. She hadn't quite hit rock bottom yet, but she knew when she did, it was going to hurt like hell.

Millie walked into Taz's hotel suite ahead of him, his words reverberating through her head. *Winning is everything.*

Winning couldn't be more important than human connections, friendships and relationships. Could it be the only thing that mattered? Surely not.

'You seem distracted,' Taz said, pulling his bowtie loose and shrugging out of his jacket.

Millie kicked off her heels, and the hem of her dress pooled on the floor. She watched him walk over to the credenza holding a variety of spirits. He lifted a crystal decanter. 'Cognac. Do you want one?'

No. What she wanted was to understand this man. To

discover what made him tick. She sat on the edge of the couch and rested her forearms on her knees. Taz walked over to the open doors leading to the balcony and infinity pool, leaned against its frame and sipped his drink. Behind him, the lights of the city twinkled with a certain smugness, confident of its place as one of the richest cities in the world.

'Did you mean what you said earlier?' she asked. Tension immediately slid into the muscles of his shoulders and broad back, and his stance widened. He lifted his glass to his lips, but he didn't turn to face her.

'Remind me…' he murmured.

This was the emotional equivalent of being slathered in volcanic-hot wax. 'You said that winning was everything, that nothing else mattered.'

He lifted one shoulder in a casual shrug. She was normally slow to anger, but his small, too-casual dismissal of her question annoyed her. Or was she really angry that, while she'd been falling for him, his priority was winning his fourth championship?

Had she seen what she wanted to see? The thought ratcheted up her temper. 'Do you believe nothing else is important? You've completed your five charity events, Taz, and raised millions for various charities. You've made a discernible difference in people's lives, and that's also worth celebrating,' she protested, desperate for his reassurance.

Was she looking for validation, for him to admit there was more to life than the De Rossi Racing team? Because if he couldn't, then what did that mean for her? It meant she'd made no impact on his life, that she was another fleeting presence, another speed bump hampering his race to victory. She'd felt like that before—too many times to count. Her entire life, she'd battled the fear that she was unworthy of being seen or valued. She wanted to matter to him—not because of what she could do for him but because of who she was. Because she was Millie.

But how much longer could she keep hoping, keep believing that she might be the exception to his iron-clad rule, when everything about him screamed that she wasn't?

He turned around slowly and resumed his same stance, his other shoulder pressed into the wall. 'I stand by what I said. Winning my fourth championship is all that matters, the only thing on my mind. Nothing, not my reputation or me playing ambassador for those charities or—' he hesitated, and in her mind she filled in the missing, unspoken word. He'd been about to say *you* and pulled back.

He looked down into his empty glass. 'Winning is everything, Millie. It *has* to be.'

His words were the confirmation of all her fears. Her temper spiked and revved, fast and high. With her parents she normally backed down and away, never able to find the words to hit back, to defend herself. But tonight, the words were searing her tongue, climbing over each other to be released. How dare he dismiss her and what they'd done, her hard work and the time they'd shared? She'd shared her body with him, told him about Ben, cried in his arms. He was pretending that none of that meant anything. That she didn't mean anything to him. She wouldn't stand for it.

Not today. Not anymore.

'No. There is more to life than winning, Taz,' she announced, pushing herself to her feet, emboldened by the surprise in his eyes and the shock on his face.

'Like what?' he drawled.

'Like making a difference, using your influence and status to shine a light on causes that need to be in the spotlight!'

He released a dismissive scoff. 'Like my brother did? Yes, he was Saint Alex in public and the devil in private.'

She waited for him to say more, and when he didn't she threw up her hands in frustration. 'You can't throw out statements like that and not explain!'

'I can. And don't raise your voice to me.'

His soft command sent her temper rocketing. 'Either explain or stop demeaning your brother.' Still nothing. Millie hauled in a deep breath and her courage. She couldn't back down now. 'Then, you leave me with no choice but to believe you are the insecure younger brother who can never keep up. That's why you act out, right? Because you can't compete.'

God, she ached. She knew that wasn't true, and every bit of her wanted him to let down those shields, to get real, to engage. But his stoic, untouchable force field stayed in place, and she wanted to howl.

But shouting would only cause him to shut down, and she needed to break through. She needed to keep her wits because, after all, she was going to war for his soul. A war she'd probably lose, but she couldn't help herself. She was done staying quiet, hanging back, swallowing her opinions and her feelings.

'We've accomplished something amazing, and I am furious that you can dismiss me and the work we've done together so easily. I've worked long, hard hours to rehab your reputation—'

'I never asked you to do it for free. You did get a million pounds out of the deal.'

How dare he make her feel so cheap. She sucked in a deep breath, then another. 'The world does not revolve around you, Taz. People work really hard, I've worked really hard to—'

'Actually, it does, Millie. I've deliberately created a life and business that does. Racing is my world.'

Her shoulders slumped. He only ever looked at life, at people, in relation to how they affected his ambitions, race standings and the championship he was so desperate to win. He had no desire or intention to make space for her or anything outside of racing. His career and business were all he cared about.

That was his choice. All she could control was her reaction.

And it was time to face reality.

She'd been pushed aside, made to feel like she was insignificant long enough. He might be an in-front-of-the-cameras man and she a behind-the-scenes woman, but she was still consequential, she was important. She had things to do and say and a life to live. His world might revolve around the De Rossi brand, but hers didn't. She wanted something more, something real, a complete man, not someone who would only share a sliver of his life, mind and soul. It wasn't enough.

She had to get out now, while she could. Before she slid back into believing that her place would always be standing in the shadow of someone more brilliant than her.

Millie pushed back her shoulders and gathered the tattered remains of her courage. 'If that's the way you feel, then I guess this is as good a time as any to tell you that I can't do this anymore, Taz.'

His eyes narrowed, trying to make sense of her words, to figure out where she was going with this. 'I'm resigning. I will stay until after the race tomorrow, but on Monday, I will no longer be running your PR or acting as your press officer. Or posing as your girlfriend. If you don't do something asinine, like losing your temper or hooking up with Phoebe again, your reputation should hold steady.'

He jerked at her words and rubbed his hand over his face. 'Look, I admit that we both said some things—'

She held up her hand. 'Don't... This isn't a negotiation, Taz. I'm done. *We're* done.'

'Millie—'

'I'm going to sleep in the bedroom, Taz. You can sleep alone and dream about the race. Maybe you'll consider what I said before, that you are racing against a ghost.' Gathering up her dignity, Millie headed for the bedroom, cradling her battered heart. At the last moment, she stopped and turned back.

'And in case you don't know this...the ghost will always win.'

CHAPTER THIRTEEN

COMPETING WITH A GHOST.

Millie's words roared through his head, and his stomach roiled, filled with anxiety, anger and a healthy dose of self-loathing. The thought of Millie leaving made his blood run hot, then cold, and then stop running entirely. The urge to run down the passage and storm into the bedroom, to gather her to him and rain kisses and apologies on her, was as strong as his urge to win his fourth championship.

He couldn't imagine her not being there and didn't know how he was going to fill the Millie-sized hole in his life. But he also couldn't allow his feelings to get in the way of what he needed to accomplish. He paced the area in front of the open door, his heart rate erratic. He'd given himself a little more leeway because he wasn't racing and had stepped away, just a fraction, but now that his hand was better and he could drive... That meant focusing on what was truly important. And that was racing.

Reaching the pinnacle of this sport, being the very best of the best, being spoken about in the same reverent terms as the greats, required insane levels of selfishness and dedication. Why couldn't Millie understand that he'd allow nothing to come between him and his goals, between him and racing? That if he shifted his focus an inch left or right, he might miss something crucial. And he wasn't only talking about his skills on the track but his management and leadership skills. This industry was filled with bright and ambitious people, men and women who would pounce on his smallest mistake. Being self-absorbed was a strength, not a weakness.

Not having any distractions was another.

He couldn't, wouldn't, let go of his focus on his dream for a woman. Not even for a woman who knew him as well as Millie did. She got him, on levels he never expected, but was she special enough for him to sacrifice his dream? No. Nobody was. Nobody would ever be.

His father never believed in him, so he had to believe in himself. Alex never respected him, so he had to have enough self-respect for both of them. He'd worked hard to get to where he was, battled his father's lack of belief and support and fought for his place in the sun, and he wouldn't surrender the ground he'd gained.

Especially not for something as vague as love. Because love was too indefinable, too much like mist fighting the sun. It couldn't be bottled or contained, anchored or corralled. Love could morph, leave; love could change. He needed ironclad guarantees.

Maybe it was better if Millie faded from his life, both business and personal. If she did, he could go back to being the driven, ambitious, fully focused boss he'd always been. He'd win the championship. It would be a hard battle, but he was the personification of determination—and then he'd settle on a new challenge, a new goal. Something fresh to chase, a mountain—literally or metaphorically—to climb.

A new race to win.

* * *

Millie stood in the press room, her thumb flicking against her front teeth as she watched the Monaco race on the big screen TV. Her heart was in her mouth because Taz was having, as the commentators kept repeating, an *inconsistent* race. There were moments of brilliance, followed by him taking a stupid risk, and then him not taking what they called *easy wins*. They were perplexed by his actions and worried he'd slip farther down the field.

Winning the race was impossible. A podium finish the longest of shots.

Her heart ached for him. Millie looked at her laptop bag, mentally reviewing everything she needed to do before exiting Taz's life tomorrow. She had struggled to write the press release stating she and Taz were splitting up, eventually settling on the tried and true *We're parting to concentrate on our careers, but we will remain good friends* hogwash. She had press releases ready to go whether he won, lost or didn't feature in this race—although the last option looked more and more likely.

Whenever she thought of Taz, it felt like her heart was on fire, every beat a struggle. Leaving him felt like she was ripping her soul in half, but what choice did she have? Staying meant questioning every moment with him, his every word, every look. Wondering if she was a priority in his life, and if he could ever love her as much as he loved racing.

And she already knew the answer. He couldn't.

She had to walk because, while she was happy not to stand in the world's spotlight, she needed to stand in his, to have his focus and attention on her. She couldn't be an afterthought. But Taz didn't care enough to make room for her in his life. She'd played her part and restored his reputation which helped his brand. She'd been the perfect fake girlfriend, and they'd enjoyed a mutually satisfying fling.

She'd gotten as much as she could from him. She'd seen a few cracks in his emotional suit of armour, fleeting moments of realness, but they didn't occur often enough, or last long enough, to convince her to stay. There were depths to him she would never know or be able to explore because he'd deliberately shut himself off from her. There was nothing she could say or do to change that.

She loved him. But love wasn't enough. Not when it was one-sided. Not when she was willing to give him her heart, her everything, and he couldn't—or wouldn't—do the same.

Leaving him was the hardest thing she'd ever done, but she had to. Because the only thing worse than walking away was staying and losing herself in the process.

Her phone pinged, and Millie pulled it from her back pocket. She squinted at the screen, seeing that her mum had texted her. That was unusual, as Millie always reached out first. They hadn't had any contact for seven or eight months.

Without opening the message, she instinctively knew what it would say, what they wanted—and that was to bask in the publicity surrounding her and Taz. Her mother didn't disappoint.

Millie, darling. We'll all be joining you in Montreal next week. Book us rooms in the same hotel you are staying with your delicious Taz. Suites preferably. Make a reservation at Vin Mon Lapin, Taz can pay.

Millie didn't hesitate, didn't second-guess herself. Her fingers flew across the keypad as she banged out her short response.

I'm not an idiot, Mum. I know I wouldn't have heard from you had I not been dating Taz De Rossi.

She wasn't anymore, but her mother didn't need to know that.

I'm *not* your ticket to publicity, I'm barely your daughter. Don't come.

Millie saw that her mother was typing a message but decided she wouldn't read it. She wasn't in the mood to be gaslighted today. Millie shoved her phone into the back pocket of her jeans, surprised at how calm she was. Had she finally learned how to emotionally disengage? To let her mum's demands and criticisms roll off her back?

Compared to losing Taz, her family's disapproval barely registered. She'd wasted enough time and energy and was done with trying to please or impress them. She was worthwhile, with or without their approval. She'd found herself, finally saw herself as Ben did. She was smart, capable and interesting, comfortable in her skin and able to walk into ballrooms or boardrooms. She no longer needed their, or anyone's, approval.

Even if Taz couldn't love her, or make space for her in his life, she was *enough*. Excitement in the commentator's voice pulled her attention back to the screen. Instead of focusing on the leader, a driver ranked way below Taz and the other contenders for the championship, the cameras were on Taz's car as he weaved in and out of the pack in the middle of the field. The standings board flashed up on the screen, and Taz had jumped from eleventh to eighth, then to fifth, and now he was in fourth place. He was on the tail of his arch-rival and beating him would give him points in the leadership race.

'If De Rossi keeps driving like this, with verve and confidence, he might take this race. Exceptional driving by an exceptional racer,' said the race analyst.

He certainly had guts, flair and focus. Millie kept her eyes glued to the screen, her heart in her mouth. She'd spend the rest of her life wishing things between them could've been different, that they could've found a way to make it work, but she wanted him to succeed.

She wanted him to win the championship because *he* wanted it. The crowd roared as Taz overtook his rival, and the commentators and crowd went into hyperdrive. The competitor regained the lead, and his supporters screamed with excitement. The two cars stayed bumper to bumper for the next few laps with Taz fighting for third place. There were a few laps to go, ten, fifteen, and Millie knew this race would go down as one of Taz's greatest.

He'd fought hard, given everything he had to it. She wished he felt the same way about her.

Around one of the longer corners, Taz saw the smallest gap to overtake the driver and gunned his car. His rival closed the gap abruptly, and Taz was between his car and the barrier, his car scraping along the concrete bollard. Taz hung on, trying to keep control of his bullet-fast car, but his rear slid sideways. He spun out, his back clipping his rival's bumper as they headed into the straight. Both cars spun twice, Taz spun again, and the commentators announced the suspension of the race. As both competitors came to a stop, the announcers started discussing who was at fault. Had Taz misjudged the gap he'd tried to squeeze through, and had it been too small? Or had the other driver been too overzealous in trying to squeeze Taz out?

What did it matter? Both men were out of the race, both drivers failed to secure much-needed points. Both would be hot-as-hell furious. Millie, panicking, ran out of the press room and sprinted to the area where his race engineers sat on the pit wall, a structure located against the fence between the pit lane and the main straight. They were in direct communication with Taz, and they would know if he was okay.

Please don't let Taz do anything stupid. Please don't let Taz lose his temper.

Millie, and the world, watched as Taz opened his door and climbed out the window of his car. What was he going to do?

Taz kept his eyes open as the car spun around, the crowds a blur and the track flipping in and out of his vision.

This, *again*. Once was unlucky, twice was becoming a habit.

As the car slowed down and he could tell he wasn't going to hit anything hard like a concrete bollard, his heart rate dropped and his grip on the wheel loosened. Another day at the office.

When the world stopped spinning, Taz rested his head on his hands on the wheel and thought he was getting a little sick of being a superfast spinning top. This could've ended badly; he could've woken up in the hospital. Or dead. And this time there would've been no Millie in his hospital room. No Millie at all.

He looked around, thinking for the first time that it was just a race, just a place in a championship that no one would care about in a few years. He wouldn't have kids or grandkids to boast about him being an ace driver, all he would have was an empire no one but him cared about.

Empires and money didn't keep you warm at night, couldn't make you laugh, weren't there when you were sick and sad or needed someone to celebrate with.

Empires crumbled. And people who tied themselves to empires did too.

He'd cheated death twice in a car lately, and for what? To prove to himself that he was better than Alex. It was such BS: He *was* better than Alex. He was as good a driver as him, and a better businessman than his dad as he'd grown the De Rossi name into a brand worth billions.

But more than that, he hadn't built it all on a lie. He wasn't one person in public and another in private. He didn't do Class A drugs, and he didn't share them with too-young girls. He respected women. He was a demanding boss, but not overly so. Okay, maybe he was, but his employees were the best paid in the business and received huge perks.

People clamoured to join his team because he had a reputation for excellence. Yes, his reputation had needed work, and Millie had restored some of its lustre. He intended to keep it that way. Oh, he'd never be Alex-in-public perfect, but he didn't need to be.

Two crashes later, and he was done trying to prove that he was better than his brother.

It was time to say goodbye to him, to loosen the hold

he and their father had on his thoughts and life. And yeah, it was time to create his legacy and to live his own life. Hopefully with Millie. If she'd forgive him for being a selfish, stubborn, self-absorbed ass.

But first, he needed to exit this car, which was hotter than the seventh circle of hell. Taz pushed his seat back, giving him a few more inches between his torso and the wheel, and pulled a lever to release the steering wheel. After dropping it onto the grass through his open window, he disconnected his harness and hauled his tense body out of the car.

His race engineer's voice cut through the buzz in his head. 'Taz, are you okay?'

He wasn't hurt, but every muscle in his body, thanks to the Gs he'd experienced, ached. 'Bit shaken, but okay.'

He heard Len's sigh of relief. 'Was it your fault or his?' he asked.

Taz considered his question, as he watched Jean-Pierre exit his car and remove his helmet. 'Does it matter? The result is the same.'

Taz looked around. The race had stopped, and the crowd was quiet; it seemed like everyone was holding their breath. He caught Jean-Pierre's wariness and realised the crowd was waiting for his response, to see how he'd deal with this latest track setback.

And because he was Taz De Rossi, he chose a response no one expected. Tucking his helmet under his arm, he walked over to Jean-Pierre and held out his hand. Surprise and shock jumped into his eyes but the man, thank God, clasped his hand.

They didn't speak, neither choosing to claim responsibility, but neither casting blame either. They met as equals, silently agreeing to instil some decency and sportsmanship into the sport and the moment.

The crowd roared its approval, and Taz took the moment to speak into his headset. 'Len, can you get a message to Millie?' he asked, his heart in his throat.

'She's standing right next to me.'

'Give her a headset,' Taz ordered. When he heard Millie's breathy, slightly panicky demand to know if he was hurt, he knew exactly what he should do.

'Mils, I need you at the press conference.'

He thought he heard her sigh of disappointment, but she rallied well and told him she'd manage it all. 'No, you don't get it,' he insisted. 'I need you there. With *me*.'

'Okay,' she replied, and he knew she didn't understand what he was trying to say. But he couldn't talk openly, not when half the crew was listening. He thought fast and said the only thing he could, a phrase nobody but her would understand. 'Mils, you were right. I'm done competing against ghosts.'

Millie stood in front of the window of their hotel suite. It was late, and the sun had long slipped behind the horizon, casting a navy pall over the city, her thoughts spinning.

She'd accompanied Taz to the press conference, but after a quick hug and him squeezing her hand, they hadn't managed to talk, mostly because he'd been besieged. It hadn't been the right time or place to talk, but it was enough for her to know that he wanted her there. Not as his PR person or press officer, but as his lover, his support system.

That was what he meant, *right*? Or had she misunderstood him?

Millie sent a nervous look down the passage of the suite, wondering how long Taz would be in the shower. When he'd led her into his suite, he'd asked her to wait, telling her he needed a little time to decompress and to wash the day away.

She walked over to the bar, lifted a decanter and poured two fingers into a crystal tumbler. The whisky was smooth and sensuous as it slid down her throat. Pausing in front of the window, she rested her hand on the cool glass and wondered what his cryptic message had meant. Could it be that he'd reconsidered her role in his life? Or was she setting herself up for more hurt?

Taz snagged the glass from her hand and lifted it to his lips. His bare feet accounted for his silent approach. Lowering the glass, he lifted his hand and gently, using his index finger, pulled a strand of hair off her cheek and tucked it behind her ear in a tender gesture.

'Let's sit, Mils,' he suggested, taking her hand and leading her over to the couch. She sat facing the view, and Taz sat next to her, his thigh and shoulder pressing against hers. He'd changed into a slouchy navy cotton sweater and straight-legged white cotton pants and hadn't bothered to shave or brush his messy hair. He looked disreputable and hot.

Millie swallowed and took a series of mental snapshots to remember later.

Taz leaned back, his palms on the wide couch behind him. 'It's been a hell of a day,' he said, and she heard the exhaustion in his voice.

'Hell of a day,' she echoed. 'How are you feeling after your crash?'

She felt his shoulder rise and fall. 'My muscles are a bit sore from tensing when I spun out, but I'm fine.'

Should she compliment him on the way he'd handled the crash and avoided a confrontation with his rival? She might as well; it wasn't like he could fire her. Well, he could, but she'd already told him she would be gone in the morning. 'You handled the disappointment well,' she murmured.

'Mmm, but two crashes in a row is ridiculous,' he muttered. 'And before you ask, my hand is fine.'

That was going to have been her next question. Having nothing else to say, she stared at the slumberous sea, conscious of the tension between them. Why was she here? What did he want? But her pride, the little she had left, wouldn't let her ask. He'd either tell her or he wouldn't. She was done begging people to let her in.

'My dad wasn't interested in me,' Taz said, his voice soft. 'I was my mum's kid, and I rarely saw him, and he and Alex were a tight unit. When my mum died when I was six, I was…*forgotten* is a good word. Ignored too. I was the third wheel.'

Millie turned to face him, blindsided by his out-of-the-blue-statement and openness. She lifted her thigh onto the couch. 'Why are you telling me this now, Taz?'

He pushed his fingers into his damp hair. 'Because you're the only one I *can* tell, Mils.'

Okay, but she was leaving in the morning. Why now?

She waited for him to speak, her eyes on his face. He looked uncomfortable but also determined, like he had a rotten tooth poisoning his system.

'Alex wasn't the charming, jovial, great guy everyone thought he was.' His words left his mouth in a rush as if he couldn't get them out fast enough. He shoved his hand into his hair and tugged the expertly cut strands. 'He was difficult, rude and often obnoxious. Entitled.'

Misery skittered across Taz's face. 'But in my father's eyes, he could do no wrong. His behaviour was excused because of his extraordinary talent at throwing cars around the track.'

It was so strange to hear about this other side of the sports hero. Knowing how hard it was for him to open up, to share this with her, Millie placed her hand on his knee and squeezed. She was still processing his words when Taz spoke again. 'I wanted to go to the same driving academy Alex attended, but my father refused to pay. I continued to beg, he continued to say no. I think he got a kick out of my desperation because, more than anything, I wanted to race.' Taz rubbed the back of his neck. 'I begged, pleaded, ranted, raged, and he eventually gave in. I think he was desperate to get me to shut up.'

He'd been desperate to go to such lengths to push his father into giving him the same opportunity he had Alex. He must've felt so lonely, battered by being consistently rejected. Her heart ached for the boy he'd been.

'My father caved. I started in F3, then was given a chance with another team at F1 level. I only moved to the De Rossi team because Ben died, and the press gave my father a hard time about not employing his other talented son.' She heard the bitterness in his voice and understood it. She'd be bitter too.

Taz fiddled with the strap of his expensive watch and twisted his leather and silver bracelet around his wrist. He looked nervous, his knee was bouncing up and down, and Millie laid her hand on his arm.

This was hard for him, and he was worried about saying too much. 'I'm still happy to sign that NDA,' she murmured, nuclear-strike serious.

'I wouldn't tell you this if I didn't trust you completely, Millie,' he replied. He held her eyes, and Millie felt like she was taking possession of his heart and soul. She tried to dislodge the tight ball in her throat by swallowing. Something was happening between them, but she wasn't sure what.

'I need to tell you about the night he died.'

She shook her head. Discussing Alex was painful, and he'd endured enough. 'You don't, Taz, because everyone knows that he slipped and hit his head.'

He released a half laugh, half snort and slid his fingers between hers, his grip tight. 'That was the end result, Millie. Nobody but my father's very expensive attorney and I know what happened before that. I want to tell you. Alex flew to New York for the weekend. His fiancée was away. He did that often. He called it Alex Time. Alex dropping off the grid was commonplace, and everyone figured he spent the weekend on his own, decompressing.' Taz dropped his head and stared at the floor. 'That weekend in New York, he didn't know my dad was staying in the Upper West Side house, that he was upstairs.'

Millie bit her lip. What was he about to tell her?

'My father heard a scream, came downstairs and saw a teenager standing in the kitchen. She was young, half-undressed and stoned. There were coke lines on the table, and they'd been drinking. She was crying. He asked where Alex was, and she pointed to him. He was on the floor. She told him he'd run to answer his phone, slipped and cracked his head open on the edge of the marble counter.' He rubbed his hand over his face. 'My dad held him while he died.'

Millie wiped away a tear. The pain in his voice made her heart ache.

In a monotone, Taz went on to explain that his dad had called his lawyer instead of 911. The attorney took him upstairs and when he allowed Matteo downstairs later, there was no sign of the drugs, alcohol or the girl. The first responders and Alex's body were gone, and the house had been cleaned. People had been paid off.

Matteo's simple explanation—that he came downstairs and found Alex on the floor with a cracked head—was accepted. It was the truth, but not the *whole* truth. After Matteo suffered his first stroke that night, somebody had been required to make decisions, to run the De Rossi empire, and he'd stepped up. When Matteo had died, Taz became the keeper of his and Alex's secrets.

Millie wrapped her arms as far as they could go around Taz's shoulders and hugged him. He buried his face in her neck for less than a minute before pulling back. 'Don't cry for someone you didn't know, Mils. It breaks my heart.'

Millie swiped her hand over her face. 'I'm crying for *you*! Nobody should have to go through that.'

He cradled her face in his hands and wiped away her tears with his thumbs. 'Do you know why I told you my biggest secret, Millie?'

She looked into his eyes, so tender, so sincere, his expression so wide open, and shook her head. 'No, I have no idea,' she whispered.

'Partly because I want you to know everything about me, both good and bad. I've never wanted that before, have always put a wall up between myself and everyone else, shown them what I wanted them to see. But it's also because I trust you, Millie. You're the first person I've told, and you'll be the last.' He smiled and kissed her nose. 'I don't want us to have any secrets going forward.'

'Going forward?' She sounded like a parrot but couldn't help it. She was struggling to catch up.

He stroked her cheek. 'You're the only one for me, Millie. You're my championship, my ultimate win. Nothing compares to having you in my life.'

She stared at him, unblinking. What was happening right now?

'Life isn't about winning races or championships or fame and fortune. Life is seeing your lovely face every morning, being able to look at you when my temper spikes but you smile and all the frustration fades away. It's about making love with you and maybe, one day, making the family neither of us had.'

Millie held his wrists, unable to believe what he was saying. She lifted an eyebrow. 'Want to run that by me again?' She needed him to keep explaining until it made sense.

His open smile liquified her knees. 'I want to be better than the man I was before, Mils. Since meeting you, I've had to up my game, and that's been the best gift anyone could've given me. I want to be a better friend, boss, partner and lover.' He sent her a look so full of admiration, love and sincerity that her knees would have buckled if she'd been standing. 'You're real and lovely and kind, occasionally feisty, and so damn patient.'

'You forgot *good in bed*.' She had to joke because if she didn't, she'd start to cry again.

His eyes turned to liquid silver. 'You're amazing in

bed.' He lifted her hand and kissed the back of her knuckles. 'And when you look at me like that, your eyes a little purple, a lot hot, I can't think about anything but getting you naked.'

She reached for him, but he shook his head and scooted down the couch, out of her reach. He held his hands up, palms facing her. 'I've still got things to say.'

There was *more*?

Taz rubbed the back of his neck. 'In my safe in my apartment in London is my mum's engagement ring. She loved it, and I want to give it to you.'

She slapped her hand on her heart. 'Oh, that's—' Wait, *what*? Why did he want to give her his mum's ring?

Taz moved off the couch and went down on one knee. What was he doing? He looked nervous, unsure. He was putting himself out there....*way* out there. Tears burned her eyes. It was so unlike Taz.

He swallowed, his cheeks pink beneath his olive skin. 'Millie, I love you. Will you be my wife?'

She cocked her head, happiness bubbling inside her. 'Pretend wife, or real wife?' she asked, a part of her needing to make sure he wasn't joking.

'My very-real, stay-with-me-forever and keep-me-out-of-trouble wife.' He looked down at the hard floor and lifted an eyebrow. 'This is the most uncomfortable position known to man, so a quick answer would be appreciated.'

She leaned forward and flung her arms around his neck. She was loved, and she'd found herself and her place. Best of all, she'd found herself before she'd found her man. She knew who she was, and that was everything.

'Yes, I'll marry you, Taz.'

Taz rested his forehead against hers. 'Thank God,' he murmured, his lips claiming hers. After a tender kiss, he pulled back and cradled the side of her face in his palm. 'You, this…it's everything. Nothing will top this moment, Millie.'

'Not even winning a fourth championship?'

Taz smiled at her. 'Not even close, sweetheart.' His voice cracked with emotion as the last of his shields disintegrated and his emotional walls collapsed. 'You're… you're my every breath, my future, the mother of my children, my best friend. God, you're *everything*.'

She was someone's—no, Taz's *everything*. And for the first time, Millie's world, and life, made complete sense.

EPILOGUE

Abu Dhabi

MILLIE STOOD IN the centre of the De Rossi Racing crew, oblivious to the celebrations happening around her. Droplets of sprayed champagne landed on her face and mingled with her tears. It was the last race of the season, and Taz, despite racing his heart out, had ended the year with the same number of points as his closest rival. But because Jean-Pierre won more races over the season, he'd snatched the world championship title from Taz at the very last moment.

De Rossi Racing winning the Constructors' Championship was great news, and Taz would be happy with that, but she'd wanted the fourth championship for him. Biting her lip, Millie watched Taz pose for photographs on the podium, looking festive and happy, his smile wide. But her fiancé was exceptionally good at hiding his real feelings from everyone but her, and she knew there was pain behind his charming grin.

Because, despite telling her he was done competing with his brother, she knew a part of him still wanted to beat Alex's record. She stamped her foot, wishing she could loudly announce that Taz De Rossi was ten times the man his brother was…in every way that counted.

But she'd promised Taz she'd keep his secrets, so she would. She wouldn't do anything, ever, to jeopardise their happiness.

Taz jumped off the stage and pushed through the people swarming him to stand in front of her. His hair was wet from the champagne, his grey eyes sparkling. He clasped her face in his hands and swiped his mouth across hers, feeding her a kiss full of love and heat…

Bending his head he spoke above the roaring crowd. 'You are looking a bit militant, my darling. What's up?'

She shook her head and wrapped her fingers around his wrist. 'I wanted you to win. You worked so hard, and you *deserved* to win.'

He shook his head, wrapped his arms around her and boosted her up. Her legs locked around his hips, and they were nose to nose, their focus on each other, both ignoring the cameras pointed in their direction.

'Are you thinking about what happened in New York?' he asked, his voice pitched just loud enough for her to hear.

She nodded and Taz shook his head. 'I'm done competing with him, Mils. I have been for months. I care about racing and the team, but it's not my reason for living anymore. You are, sweetheart.' He lifted his hand to drag his thumb over her cheekbone, to let it rest in the middle of her bottom lip. His eyes radiated sincerity, and Millie knew that he was well and truly done with competing with Alex. That their relationship, their amazing life, was all that mattered and was his highest priority.

She brushed her nose against his. Millie had no doubt

how much she was loved, but because occasionally she needed a little additional assurance, in a teasing tone she said, 'Prove it.'

His eyes remained locked on hers, intensely determined, very Taz. 'I swear I will. Every day, for the rest of my life, Mils. I also promise to love you more tomorrow than I did today, more the next day than I will tomorrow…you get the picture.'

That was a *lot* of love. Her eyes burned with unshed happy tears, and Millie pulled him closer. The world around them faded. The cameras, the noise, all of it disappeared as his mouth claimed hers, sealing his promises with a kiss that tasted like forever.

* * * * *

Did Fast-Track Dating Deception *leave you enthralled? Then don't miss Joss Wood's other dazzling stories!*

The Nights She Spent with the CEO
The Baby Behind Their Marriage Merger
Hired for the Billionaire's Secret Son
A Nine-Month Deal with Her Husband
The Tycoon's Diamond Demand

Available now!

Get up to 4 Free Books!

We'll send you 2 free books from each series you try PLUS a free Mystery Gift.

FREE Value Over $25

Both the **Harlequin Presents** and **Harlequin Medical Romance** series feature exciting stories of passion and drama.

YES! Please send me 2 FREE novels from Harlequin Presents or Harlequin Medical Romance and my FREE gift (gift is worth about $10 retail). After receiving them, if I don't wish to receive any more books, I can return the shipping statement marked "cancel." If I don't cancel, I will receive 6 brand-new larger-print novels every month and be billed just $7.19 each in the U.S., or $7.99 each in Canada, or 4 brand-new Harlequin Medical Romance Larger-Print books every month and be billed just $7.19 each in the U.S. or $7.99 each in Canada, a savings of 20% off the cover price. It's quite a bargain! Shipping and handling is just 50¢ per book in the U.S. and $1.25 per book in Canada.* I understand that accepting the 2 free books and gift places me under no obligation to buy anything. I can always return a shipment and cancel at any time. The free books and gift are mine to keep no matter what I decide.

Choose one: ☐ **Harlequin Presents Larger-Print** (176/376 BPA G36Y)   ☐ **Harlequin Medical Romance** (171/371 BPA G36Y)   ☐ **Or Try Both!** (176/376 & 171/371 BPA G36Z)

Name (please print)

Address   Apt. #

City   State/Province   Zip/Postal Code

Email: Please check this box ☐ if you would like to receive newsletters and promotional emails from Harlequin Enterprises ULC and its affiliates. You can unsubscribe anytime.

> ### Mail to the **Harlequin Reader Service:**
> **IN U.S.A.:** P.O. Box 1341, Buffalo, NY 14240-8531
> **IN CANADA:** P.O. Box 603, Fort Erie, Ontario L2A 5X3

Want to explore our other series or interested in ebooks? Visit www.ReaderService.com or call 1-800-873-8635.

---

*Terms and prices subject to change without notice. Prices do not include sales taxes, which will be charged (if applicable) based on your state or country of residence. Canadian residents will be charged applicable taxes. Offer not valid in Quebec. This offer is limited to one order per household. Books received may not be as shown. Not valid for current subscribers to the Harlequin Presents or Harlequin Medical Romance series. All orders subject to approval. Credit or debit balances in a customer's account(s) may be offset by any other outstanding balance owed by or to the customer. Please allow 4 to 6 weeks for delivery. Offer available while quantities last.

Your Privacy—Your information is being collected by Harlequin Enterprises ULC, operating as Harlequin Reader Service. For a complete summary of the information we collect, how we use this information and to whom it is disclosed, please visit our privacy notice located at https://corporate.harlequin.com/privacy-notice. Notice to California Residents – Under California law, you have specific rights to control and access your data. For more information on these rights and how to exercise them, visit https://corporate.harlequin.com/california-privacy. For additional information for residents of other U.S. states that provide their residents with certain rights with respect to personal data, visit https://corporate.harlequin.com/other-state-residents-privacy-rights/.

HPHM25